LOVE AT FIRST FLIGHT

Bisi Abejo

Spectrum Books limited
Ibadan • Owerri • Kaduna • Lagos

Published by
Spectrum Books Limited
Sunshine House
1, Emmanuel Alayande Street
Oluyole Industrial Estate
P.M.B. 5612
Ibadan, Nigeria

in association with
Safari Books (Export) Limited
Bel Royal House
Hilgrove Street
St. Helier, Jersey
Channel Islands, UK

Europe and USA Distributor
African Books Collective Ltd.,
The Jam Factory,
27 Park End Street,
Oxford OX1, 1HU, UK

© Bisi Abejo, 1986

First Published 1986
Reprinted 1996

ISBN 978-246-000-1

Printed by Printmarks, Ibadan

Chapter One

Many heads turned to look at the tall slender girl, as spurning the moving centre corridor, she walked towards the final transit lounge prior to boarding the giant jet. It wasn't her beauty that was so arresting for, as she would have been the first to admit, her limpid brown eyes were too large and her generously full mouth too wide for the proportions of her face for true beauty. It wasn't the cool elegance of her crisp cream suit, worn with a pure silk crepe de chine shirt in warmer tones that complimented the light hue of her complexion. Nor was it the sight of her long slender legs as she stepped out briskly, a practicable but elegant brown leather bag swinging from her shoulder as she walked. Nor was it the shine on her soft black curls, caught in the dying rays of sunlight streaming in through the windows.

It was the aura of happiness that surrounded her that attracted their attention. Her piquant face shone and it was as if she were lit up with it. There was a confidence in her light springy step that only comes from within. She looked as if the whole world was her oyster. This inner glow, burning so brightly made her seem like a bright flame and it warmed and charmed everyone about her.

So wrapt up in her obviously happy thoughts was she, that she was totally unaware of the interest she aroused. Once into the final lounge she sat down, put her neat cabin bag at her feet and looked around her.

The lounge was fast filling up. Soon, she guessed they would start loading the aircraft. They were a mixed bunch of passengers — Europeans and Africans, young, old, fat and thin. Some of the Nigerians were in their native costumes, making her feel excited and happy. She really was on her way home! Some were in smart European clothes, as Cecilia was. Most of the Europeans in tropical suits looked like business men, but some were obviously going back from leave. They were more casually dressed in open-necked sports shirts and jeans. Not for them the neat executive brief cases of the business men; they had parcels of all shapes and sizes, carrier bags and large, lumpy hold-alls.

Suddenly Cecilia's eyes lit upon the man who had just walked in, and was standing motionless, looking around him. He was the most handsome man that she had ever seen — handsome and unbearably arrogant with it, probably a male chauvinist too.

He was well over six feet tall, with broad shoulders and slim hips. He stood there, tall and proud, coolly looking over his fellow passengers. Then, his eyes lighting on Cecilia, he slowly but deliberately moved towards her, a confident smile turning up the corners of his strong mouth and making a network of laughter lines round his brightly piercing dark brown eyes.

Cecilia groaned to herself. Oh, why had she looked at him. He must have noticed her gaze and that must be why he was making a bee-line for her. He might be good looking and the answer to some maiden's prayer, but he was the sort of macho type of he-man that she detested. He sat down on the empty seat next to her and a whiff of tantalisingly male after-shave reached her nostrils. Very pointedly she opened the magazine on her lap, and kept her eyes glued to the pages, but not before she had caught his insolent look, as he brazenly appraised her, stripping her of her clothes with his glance.

Cecilia was used to coping with eager males and could give them the brush-off politely, but very efficiently, but she sensed that this man sitting beside her was no ordinary male. She just hoped that he was travelling first class, which, judging from the cut of his American cotton suit, with its fine navy pin stripe on a white background, his exquisitely embroidered shirt that could only have come from the Phillipines, and the elegant hand-luggage he carried, he most likely was.

"You must be a slow reader, "said a lazy deep voice, with a hint of amusement in it," you really should have turned the page by now. That is if you really are reading that article."

Cecilia was furious, as much with herself as with him. True, she hadn't been reading the article, she had been thinking about him, and he knew it. Drat him! He probably thought that she was overcome by his superb physique and the aura of masculine virility that surrounded him. Well, she would show him! She would start as she meant to go on. She lifted up her head slowly and looked coldly at him. It was a look that would have withered most men. "I fail to see what business it is of yours," she said, her voice as icy as she could make it.

"None at all," he replied easily. "It's just that I am surprised that a young woman like you needs to study so intently the advice in that article." His eyes were glinting mockingly at her and he was grinning widely.

Cecilia looked down at the page open before her. "How to be sexy and fat," was the caption that met her eyes! She slammed the magazine shut. Damn him! She felt like getting up and moving elsewhere, but pride would not allow her.

"That's better, now we can talk. Talking passes the time much better on a journey, don't you agree?" He grinned disarmingly at her, and she was aware that he could be devastatingly attractive if he wished. But not to me, she thought, and instinctively twisted the small diamond and ruby engagement ring on her finger. His eyes followed the movement. Perhaps that will put him off thought Cecilia, not deigning to answer his remarks. But he went on imperturbably. "Of course you may be the modern sort of career young woman who prefers to work on a journey, but I surmise you are going home — to get married perhaps? Anyway, you are much too lovely to fit into the first category, thank heavens."

Cecilia could not keep silent. Really the man was impossible! "Then you would be wrong. True I am going back to Nigeria, that much is obvious, and true I am going to meet up with my fiancé, but I do happen to be the sort of woman that you seem to despise so much."

"I don't despise them, I meet with quite a few in my line of work, and I treat them like men. They just don't appeal to me at all, as women, if you see what I mean." He replied unruffled, raising one dark eye-brow sardonically. "Whereas you strike me as being all woman, capable of fire and emotion, although I must say you are behaving a little sulkily at the moment."

The blood rose to Cecilia's cheeks, as leaping up, she picked up her hand baggage and turned on him, "You are insufferably insulting and just what I expected when I saw you standing so arrogantly when you came in. I . . . "

"That is why I came over to you. I noticed this

5

beautiful woman looking me up and down with such passionate brown eyes so I came over to give her a better chance to appraise me." He was openly laughing at her now. And, damn the man, he was far too observant. She had been appraising him, but not favourably, as he so obviously thought.

"Yes, I was looking at you, and for your information as you seem to think that you are God's gift to women, was thinking that you are the type of man that I most abhor. It comes as no surprise to me that you are the complete male chauvinist who regards women as play-things, and those whom you can't put into that category you treat as men. Thank heavens my fiancé is not like you. He's proud of my work and respects me for it." Cecilia drew herself up to her full height, adding coldly, "So, if you will forgive me, I will sit elsewhere as you and I have obviously nothing to say to each other."

His mouth tightened momentarily, and Cecilia got a brief glance of another kind of man: a man as hard as granite, a man who would get his way at all costs, a man made to be at the top. He too rose to his feet, and as he towered over her she felt little frissons of fear run through her body. He held her gaze for a moment, which seemed minutes to Cecilia. His deep-set eyes seemed to bore into her soul, little flames of anger flickering in them. But then he smiled, and a small sigh of relief escaped through her closed lips, as the moments of tension between them relaxed.

6

"I hope we shall meet again, Miss . . . .?" His voice ended on a question mark which Cecilia deliberately ignored.

"I hope not," she replied sweetly, as she walked away to sit beside a mother with three young children.

"Do you need any help?" she asked the harrassed woman.

"Oh, thank you! I was just wondering how I was going to manage. If you wouldn't mind carrying that bag for me when they call us onto the plane, it would be a great help."

Even when, about twenty minutes later, Cecilia found her seat in the plane and stowed her cabin bag in the locker overhead, she was still feeling ruffled. She fastened her safety belt, then leaning her head back against the seat shut her eyes and deliberately thought about Tim and the new post she was to take up, working on the same project as he. A little smile turned up the corners of her mouth, as she thought how surprised he had been to find that she too had got a job at the Research College of Agriculture. True, his letter in reply to this news had disappointed her. He had sounded very surprised. Unflatteringly so, considering her qualifications and the fact that they had always planned to work together eventually, when they got married. All she had done by getting this job, was to bring the marriage closer. She had deliberately not mentioned Tim's name at her interview with the Provost of the College. She was determined to get the job on her own merits or not at all. She knew that females working in her field were still pretty rare: it was still very much a man's world. She had admired the Provost enormously for his completely unprejudiced views. She had the best qualifications of all the candidates, with her Ph.D in Biological Pest Control, and he had told her afterwards, she had interviewed very well. So here she was, her cup of happiness filled to over-flowing, on her way to join her fiancé, and to a much sought after post at RCA. And she was going back home as well. A girl couldn't ask for more! She gave a sigh of pure contentment, and wishing to live with her thoughts for a little longer, kept her eyes shut as she moved her body into an even more comfortable position. But she was rudely brought back to the present by an already familiar masculine voice saying, "Princesses don't sigh when they are really asleep, and just when I was about to wake you with a kiss too."

Cecilia sat bolt upright, her lovely eyes wide open with astonishment and annoyance. "Really you are impossible. Go and take your first class seat and leave me alone." His long body was leaning over her as he made himself as small as possible to let another passenger pass him in the narrow passage, and she found it unnerving.

"I'm sorry to disappoint you, but I am not in the First Class." He smiled down at her disarmingly. It was a devastating smile, and a lesser person would have been melted by it, but it just made Cecilia angrier than ever.

"Then go and find your seat wherever it is. Can't you see you are making a nuisance of yourself standing there blocking the gangway?" She saw an air hostess coming up the aisle, "I wonder if you could help this gentleman to find his seat? He seems unable to do so on his own," Cecilia asked the girl, giving her a charming smile. Without a murmur, the man held up his boarding pass with his seat number attached and handed it to the air hostess with a smile, that obviously did devastate, judging from the girl's reactions.

"But he has found it, Miss, "she said, when she had looked at the seat number, and then added rather enviously, "It is that empty seat next to yours." She gave the man a big smile that contained more than a hint of an invitation. It was at once returned by him in answering manner.

"There must be some mistake, "Cecilia's voice was sharp with exasperation." This ..." she paused, "gentleman, cannot possibly have this seat. I am sure his is in the First Class."

The Air Hostess replied firmly, "This is the right seat, Miss," and with another flirtatious smile at the tall, rangy, God-like specimen, she departed.

Words failed Cecilia, who was usually never at a loss for them. She tucked her legs in to let him go by. She was blowed if she would get up for him – No way! She realised her mistake as his body brushed past her and her own responded with strange tinglings.

This is totally ridiculous, she told herself. A mature young woman like me letting a complete stranger get under my skin to the point of making me furious, and then making me tingle from casual physical contact with his body. Quite ridiculous! She picked up the In-Flight magazine, totally ignoring his polite, "Thank you," as he slid his large frame into the seat beside her. She would make it quite clear that she did not want to talk.

He seemed to get the message and kept quiet, but just the feel of him sitting there disturbed her strangely. Even if he didn't speak to her, she couldn't be completely free of him. But it was too much to hope that he would keep quiet for long. As soon as the mighty jet had roared along the runway and started its ascent into the evening sky, his voice once again broke into her reverie. She had been trying to decide whether to have *Miss Dior* or *L'Air du Temps* from the duty free trolley, when it came along.

"What a bit of luck that I should get this seat next to you," he said, pleasantly.

"I am not sure that I would call it luck. Your type can fix anything," Cecilia retorted hotly, forgetting her resolve to maintain silence. He looked at her with a shocked expression, "I can't think what you mean," he said.

"Then I'll spell it out for you. You are the sort

of plane pest who will bribe someone to get the seat you want. I know your sort!" Cecilia glared at him.

"My dear young lady, how could I do that when I was given my seat before I had set eyes on you?" He looked guilelessly into her large eyes.

"Well, I don't know how it is done. I only know that it is," Cecilia said, stubbornly. At that moment the chief steward stopped beside them, "That seat all right for you, Sir? Sorry that we couldn't find room for you in the First Class, but as you know First Class gets booked up months beforehand on this route."

Cecilia seized her small moment of triumph. "I was right! You are a first class passenger. Too bad you have to slum it back here in Economy." She was pleased to see that she had got under his armour, as his mouth tightened. "As it happens, I often travel Economy, and I do not feel that I am slumming." His eyes had become hard as ebony, and once again she felt little shivers of fear go through her. It irritated her. She was definitely not used to any man, let alone a mere stranger, having this effect on her emotions. On the contrary, even with Tim she complimented herself on her emotional control. It was due to her scientific background, she had told herself.

"As for this seat, as you can see, it is in the row that has most leg-room. I always ask for it when I travel Economy." The hardness left his eyes to be replaced with an almost apologetic smile.

Cecilia looked around and saw that what he said was the truth. Of course he would ask for this row, with his long legs. She felt acutely embarrassed, realising that she had made a complete fool of herself. "I'm sorry," she said stiffly. "I don't know what to say, I. . ."

"There is no need to say anything." He placed a hand gently across hers. "Lets forget about it. We got off to a bad start that's all. I shall get you a drink and . . ."

"No, thank you. Really there is no need for you to do that."

"But I want to. I want us to drink to the burying of the hatchet." He smiled disarmingly. His face was so close to hers that she felt the full force of the magnetism of the man.

Steeling herself against it, and all it implied of his latent sexuality, she made a quick, scientific survey of his face. Short black curls framed a broad forehead, high cheek bones and a ruggedly determined jaw. His nose was strong, but there was a sensitivity about the wide, flaring nostrils, giving him the air of a thoroughbred arab stallion. A fine mixture of strength, breeding, and temperament. The mouth, now smiling so widely, high-lighted the sensual grooves that ran down between nose and cheeks. It was a treacherous mouth, Cecilia decided, for when it was smiling it completely disarmed, hiding the steely quality she already knew to lie beneath.

"Well?" he questioned, and she was not sure if he was referring to his suggestion of a drink to bury the hatchet, or if he was aware of her lightening appraisal of his face. She lowered her eyes, feeling the blood rushing to her cheeks.

"Thanks you, I'll drink to that. Not that it is important," she added coolly, "as we are hardly likely to see each other again." Much better to be casually polite to him and then to disappear when they landed. So when he asked her name, she omitted her surname. "Cecilia," she said, accepting the glass of champagne that he had poured for her.

"Ezeilo," he replied, raising his glass to her. "Bury the hatchet?" he asked, smilingly.

"Bury the hatchet," she replied.

"That is much better. You look enchanting when you lose your temper, but much more so when you smile." His eyes twinkled with merriment, and inspite of herself she burst out laughing.

"You and I can have nothing in common. Our views on everything must be quite opposite, I feel sure," Cecilia said, after she had sipped the deliciously dry champagne.

"You look enchanting when you are being serious too," Ezeilo interrupted. "Do you like the champagne?" She nodded, "Delicious, thank you."

"There, you see. There is at least one thing we are in agreement about. "He lifted the bottle to fill up her glass.

"No, please, no more. I don't want to meet my

fiancé the worse for alcohol. And only a small amount flies to my head."

He didn't press her. She had to give him that. Instead he refilled his own glass. "This fiancé of yours, is he worthy of you?" His eyes were looking at her intently. She met his gaze firmly. "Of course he is. And we have so much in common to base our life together on."

"Do you always take such a practical view of life?" he queried.

"Yes", Cecilia said. "I do". And with good reason, she thought. Her parents went through life from one emotional high to another and their constant rows were just as much emotional highs to them as their happy moments. As a child Cecilia had been torn to bits by their noisy, hurtful rows and in the end they had torn themselves to pieces. That they had loved each other she didn't doubt, but that had not been enough to overcome their total incompatability. Cecilia had sworn that she would never marry for emotional reasons alone. She would use the good brain that God had given her and choose sensibly. Friendship must be the basis of a happy marriage, she had decided. That and common interests which should make for compatability. She had all that with Tim.

"What a pity!" Ezeilo sighed.

"Why?" she questioned, bristling. "I think it is the only intelligent way to look at it." She handed her empty glass to the stewardess, who was collecting

14

them, prior to dinner being served.

He shook his head, "Not for you. For some under-sexed intellectual perhaps." His eyes raked her figure and lingered where, exposed by the cut of her blouse, a little gold cross nestled in the hollow between the lovely curves of her firm young breasts.' He continued, "Not for a beautiful, highly emotional, sexy lady like you." His eyes had now fixed on her lips and for one wild moment, Cecilia thought he was going to kiss her in front of the whole cabin. She pulled as far away from him as possible, leaning into the aisle. "You must be looking at someone else. I assure you that that description does not fit me at all," she said coldly.

"I think a sexy lady's is a very apt description. You see an undersexed girl would not have jumped to the conclusion that she was in danger of being kissed, just now. You got the message loud and clear, didn't you, Cecilia?" He ran a fingertip down her cheek, sending curious tremors through her body." I think, however, as a I didn't kiss you, however much I may have wanted to, you had better stop leaning right out into the aisle as the poor stewardness wants to get through with the dinner trolley." His lips twitched into a grin.

Damn the man! He was playing with her like a cat with a mouse. Come to think of it he looked rather like a big black cat. A panther, Cecilia decided, and with as much dignity as she could muster, she sat upright in her seat again.

The arrival of dinner gave her a little respite, as Ezeilo tucked into his food as if he hadn't eaten a good meal for days. The meal was delicious. They had both chosen the roast leg of lamb, as Ezeilo had said that it would be the last they would see for sometime. It had been one of Cecilia's favourite meals in the UK so she had been happy to comply with his suggestion — this once! There was smoked salmon for starters and with the beautifully cooked lamb, roast potatoes, and cauliflower in a delicious cheese sauce were served. To round off the meal, there was a creamy trifle followed by cheese and biscuits. It was a lovely meal. All the same Cecilia was looking forward to good home cooking and childhood favourites.

Ezeilo wiped his mouth on the table napkin provided, and sat back with a sigh of contentment.

"You like European food, I see," Cecilia remarked with a smile. She had had no room left for her cheese and biscuits, but he had eaten hers as well as his own. He shook his head, "Not particularly, but truth to tell I've been travelling for days now, and although most of the food provided by the airlines was all right, there was never enough of it for me, I'm afraid. But I can't wait to get home to a good pepper soup. My steward knows exactly what I like."

Cecilia had no intention of falling into the trap of asking where home was. She was determined that this acquaintanceship should go no further than the plane they were on. There was a silence while the stewardess cleared the trays. Then they put their seats back into the reclining position and Cecilia plugged in her headphones to listen to some music before the film. A large arm was suddenly thrust across her body and long fingers un-plugged the headphones from their socket in the arm of her seat.

"What on earth do you think you are doing?" she asked, crossly.

"I am un-plugging your headphone because I want to talk to you," Ezeilo answered blandly, as if what he had done was quite normal. "When the film comes on I shall let you watch, it, don't worry. I like watching films too."

"And does everyone have to do exactly as you like?" Cecilia grabbed angrily for her headphone lead which he held out of reach. "Give me back my headphones or I shall call a stewardess," Cecilia almost shouted at him.

"Do you know that your hair dances most becomingly when you shake your head in anger," Ezeilo remarked, quite unperturbed. "Call a stewardess if you like, but you will have to keep calling one every few minutes for I shall un-plug your phones as soon as her back is turned." He grinned down at her and then grabbed her hand as she made another lunge for her headphone lead.

Cecilia felt her wrist caught in a steely grip. She was furious. How dare he behave in such a high-handed manner with her! But short of a fight, which she was sure she would lose, there was nothing to it but to give in. "Please release my wrist," she requested, with as much dignity as she could muster. "As you are stronger and obviously much more selfish than I, and have no good side to your nature that I might appeal to, I shall have to give in to your brutish behaviour."

"That's my girl," he said, irritatingly, as, before she could stop him, he had chucked her under the chin. Cecilia's eyes flashed with fury. Oh, how she longed to slap him! "You are utterly impossible," she said, between clenched teeth.

"I know," he answered unruffled, "but then look where it gets me." He grinned at her and inspite of herself she felt her anger cool. Mentally she gave herself a good shake. What was the matter with her? He was an obnoxious male chauvinist if ever she saw one, and he was completely disrupting the calm journey she had planned for herself.

There was a pause for a few moments during which she was acutely conscious of his gaze upon her. He's a much deeper person than he makes himself out to be, Cecilia thought, observing him observing her, beneath her half-closed eyelids. Not that it was of any interest to her.

"Well, say something. I thought you had agreed that we should talk, "Ezeilo whispered in her ear.

"I did not say anything about talking. I just gave way to your brute force and have forgone the pleasure of listening to some pleasant music," she retorted sharply, very much aware of the closeness of his face to hers, and the tang of his after-shave, mixed with the primitive male scent that was all his own.

"All right then, it will have to be question time. I'll begin," he said good humouredly. "Cecilia what?"

She wished he'd move a little further away. She felt suffocated by his rich aura of masculinity. Suffocated she might be, but thank heavens her brain was still working. "I told you that I never wish to see you again when I get off this plane, so who I am can be of no interest to you". He tried another tack. "Your fiancee has an interesting job, has he?"

She smiled sweetly. "If you think that by talking about my fiance you will find out more about me, you underestimate me. But, yes, he has an interesting job and it so happens that I am going to join him on it. Does that satisfy you?"

"No, it doesn't. You see I don't approve of engaged women working," he answered, suddenly serious.

"They should put you in a museum. You really are the complete chauvinist aren't you?" Cecilia said, coldly.

"You could say that I suppose, but I know I have good reason for what I said. Unlike men, women get completely wrapped up in engagements and marriage, and consequently do not give value for money."

"Oh really! What arrant nonsense! And what a sweeping generalisation." Cecilia allowed the scorn to show in her voice.

"Love is everything to a woman, it's only a part of a man's life. Everyone knows that," Ezeilo answered her.

"Well let me tell you. You have just met one woman who definitely doesn't agree with you. I shall be just as efficient in my job as before." Cecilia was beginning to lose her temper. The man, was really unbelievable.

"If you would just tell me what the job was, I might be able to agree with you." He was completely unruffled.

"Oh, no! I'm not falling for that. But whatever my job is, I am just as efficient at it as any blue-stocking, as you call them."

"Ah, but then you are obviously a paragon among women." He let his eyes linger once more on the little cross nestling in the hollow between her breasts. Cecilia felt herself burn with annoyance — the audacity of the man!

"I can't say that you are a paragon of a man," she said brutally. For a moment she could have sworn that his expressive eyes had registered hurt. Then looking down at her with a serious expression on his face, he said, "I may not be a paragon among men, but I am a hard task-master. Anyone who doesn't pull his or her weight on my team is soon

20

out of a job."

Gone was his bantering tone of voice, the one that he probably kept for dalliance with the opposite sex. For that was obviously all he thought they were good for. For a moment she felt the authority of the man. There was a hard core to him. Working for him would be no sinecure.

His manner changed abruptly again, as he leant forward, and before Cecilia realised what he was doing, he had brushed his lips lightly across her ear. "Has anyone ever told you that you have ears like little dainty shells?" he murmured, "Lets not be too serious. If you are so determined that there is to be no future for us, we can at least enjoy the present. I always feel in a sort of limbo when I'm flying, totally divorced from reality."

"Is that why you behave like you do?" Cecilia moved her head away to a safe distance. She found his nearness very disturbing. She had never known anyone with such power to play upon her emotions. Those emotions that she so prided herself on having under control.

"Perhaps," he said lightly, "but it's not on every flight that I meet someone as attractive as you."

Cecilia didn't know how to cope with the situation, so it was with relief that she saw the duty-free trolley reach their row. She busied herself with finding her passport and traveller's cheques in readiness for her transactions. She decided on *Miss Dior* for herself and bought Tim an extravagant after-shave and some cigarettes, although she didn't really approve of his smoking. Ezeilo bought some after-shave and several bottles of perfume. She had bought the more economical eau de toilette. Besides it was nicer than perfume in a hot climate: one could afford to splash it all over oneself after a shower.

After that, the cabin lights were put out and the film was started. Cecilia heaved a sigh of relief, when without protest she was allowed to plug in her head set. The film, was good in parts and Cecilia found herself watching bits and then dozing off. Once, she awoke to find her head comfortably resting on Ezeilo's chest, with his arm around her. He looked as if he were asleep, but when she tried to move, his arm tightened it's a grip.

"Let go of me," she whispered, so as not to disturb the other listeners. Reluctantly he withdrew his arm. "A pity," he sighed.

Towards the end of the film, her interest was caught. It was very moving when the hero and heroine got together at last after so many misunderstandings, and Cecilia could not stop a tear from drifting down her cheek. She always reacted emotionally to films. This never worried her as she felt it was a harmless emotional outlet.

She tried furtively to wipe away the tear, but too late. Ezeilo had already seen it, and with a gentle hand turned her face towards him. He kissed away the tear with tender lips. As he pulled back,

22

their eyes locked together, neither having the power to look away. Then with a groan he held her close and ravaged her lips with his. For a second her lips responded of their own volition, and then she pushed him away angrily, "You are despicable, you know that I am engaged. How dare you do that! How dare you!"

She was more shaken than she cared to admit, even to herself, for she had felt his kiss down to her toes.

"I'm sorry, very sorry," Ezeilo apologised, seriously, "I never meant. . . ."

"And so you should be sorry," Cecilia spat out at him, her temper really roused, as much by her own reactions to his kiss as by the kiss itself. "You have subjected me to every possible kind of sexual harrassment in the book. The only thing you haven't done is to pinch my bottom."

"I'm sorry. I only meant it to be a bit of fun, and most girls enjoy it as much as I do."

"I am not — most girls. I hope I never set eyes on you again."

His lips tightened grimly, "I've apologised," he said, quietly.

"And you think that is enough? Kindly don't say another word to me, for I do not wish to speak to you."

Ezeilo did not make any further attempt to speak to her. She felt strangely deflated.

In the crush waiting to disembark, Cecilia felt a

firm pinch on her behind — but she couldn't be sure that it was him.

The last she saw of him was his back, as with long easy strides he made his way to Immigration and Customs.

Chapter Two

By the time Cecilia had got through all the formalities, her clothes were already sticking to her body, inspite of the air-conditioning in the terminal. But it was even steamer, when surrounded by a milling throng of excited people waiting to meet friends and relations, she searched for Tim. His blonde hair would have been easy to spot if it had been there, as there were few Europeans among the crowds. But search as she could, she could not see it. She hadn't expected her familiy to meet her. Infact she had insisted that they didn't as they lived in Enugu. She would go home later, as she was longing for them to meet Tim and he to meet them.

Gradually she became aware that among the crowd there were one or two placards being held up. Searching them, she found her name, Dr. Onochie, and RCA written underneath. With a sigh of relief she made her way towards the short man in uniform who was holding up the placard.

"I'm Dr. Onochie," she told the man.

"Welcome back to Nigeria, Doctor. I'm Sunday, the driver sent to take you to RCA. Just follow me, please." He took her luggage from her trolley and she gladly followed him, as he pushed his way through the crowded airport.

As they passed through the automatic doors that led to the road outside, Cecilia felt the heat hit her like a physical blow, and quickly rid herself of her costume jacket.

"Wait here please, Doctor, while I fetch the car. It may take long, but I'll be back," and with a friendly smile, he was gone.

Cecilia looked about her. It was barely light and the long, straight double carriage way that led to the airport was still blazing with lights. The road split into two outside the massive terminal building, and curving elegantly, rose to the level on which Cecilia was now standing. She took a deep breath as she looked around her. Funny how each international airport looked very much like all the others; only, she had discovered during her travels, the scent of each country was quite different, especially in the Third World which hadn't yet become uniform due to industrialisation. The air was heavy with moisture here, and so retained its scent more than in a drier clime. She found it familiar and exciting at the same time — she was back home at last!

Even her great disappointment in not finding Tim here to meet her, could not dampen her excitement on being home. But it would have been heightened by Tim's presence. Still, he had told her in his letters, that the Group Director, Doctor Obi, was a very hard task master and although he travelled quite a bit, he saw to it that the rest of the group didn't. Cecilia had the impression that this Obi was a work-a-holic and a bit of a pain in the neck. On the other hand, to be fair, the provost had sung his praises, so he obviously thought him a good guy.

A loud hoot on a car horn brought Cecilia back to earth, and she slipped into the back of the car. She heaved a sigh of relief. It was cool and dry in the car, thanks to the air-conditioning. "How long will it take us, Sunday?" she asked.

"About two hours if no go-slow, Doctor. We'll travel by the Express Way to Ibadan, and then we are nearly there." He glanced over his shoulder, "But we can stop at our Rest House, here in Lagos, if you want freshen up or have some food."

Cecilia shook her head. "No thanks, I had breakfast on the plane. I think I would rather go straight to the Campus."

"Very well Doctor," Sunday replied, and settled down to concentrate on the driving.

Driving was slow in Lagos, and it allowed Cecilia to look around her. How the place teemed with life, so early in the morning too. She'd forgotten how early people rose here. How colourful it was too, after the drabness of the UK — no gaily patterned Java prints or laces there. She looked with fresh eyes at the enormous loads the market women and children carried on their heads. Such an assortment of things, from fire-wood to food and cigarettes. She'd never taken much notice before, taking it for granted as you do things you are brought up amongst. The Taxis! Hundreds of taxis and danfo's being driven by what could only be mad men, as they appeared to ignore every rule of the road. They made her nervous. My, but I have got used to an orderly, quiet life, she thought wryly.

There was a heavy grey mist over everything, to be expected in the early dry-season mornings. Just as well too. If the sun shone for as many hours as it did on a fine English summer's day, the place and its people would be fried alive.

The mist persisted all the way on the Express Way, making the tall, dark, lush vegetation that lined the route look even darker, and very mysterious. Africa living up to it's reputation, Cecilia thought, looking out of the window as they flew along. Sunday was a very fast driver she had discovered, and was totally undeterred by the heavy mist once on the open road.

Like most motorways it was impersonal and gave the impression that there were no towns or villages, or even people living on its route. So it wasn't until they reached the outskirts of Ibadan, and were on the by-pass that skirted the city that she saw habitation again. She looked about her with interested eyes for she had never been to Ibadan. She had schooled in Enugu and then taken her first degrees at Nsuka. Ibadan was vast: as far as the eye could see there were buildings, mostly single storey houses of red mud bricks with rustly tin roofs, but some smarter two or three storeyed cement block houses. In the distance she could see a huddle of very tall office blocks, one shimmering gold in the sun.

"Is that the centre of the city, Sunday?" Cecilia asked.

"Yes, Doctor," he replied, "and you see that fine fine gold building?"

"Yes. It certainly does look fine," Cecilia replied.

"That," said Sunday, with as much pride in his voice as if he had built it himself, "that be Broking House. Latest big office block, cost plenty plenty money."

" I can imagine. And what's that taller building near it?"

"That be sad-o." he shook his head, "That be famous Cocoa House. Big fire there, every floor burning. I go see it with my own eyes." His serious expression lifted and his mouth broke into a grin. "They repair it. It be better now, but it be costing plenty plenty money to repair."

Cecilia couldn't help but smile, Sunday was quite a character.

Nothing had prepared her for the RCA campus,

the opposite of the crowded streets of Lagos and Ibadan. The car turned into a drive lined by decorative palms, smooth green grass at their feet. They were stopped by security, but once Sunday was recognised, they were waved on through the gates. Cecilia gave a little gasp of pleasure at the sight that met her eyes. The road still lined with the graceful palms, wound up a gentle hill, bouganvilleas of all colours cascading down the hedge along the left, while flowering casia trees of purple and yellow were dotted all over the campus and gradually took over the lining of the road from the decorative palms.

In a few hundred yards they drove up to a pleasant looking building, with a shimmering inviting swimming pool beside it. Sunday stopped the car and came round to let Cecilia out.

"Mr Baker said to tell you that you were to stay here until he came." As he mentioned Mr. Baker s name, Sunday looked very embarrassed and fished in his pocket, finally withdrawing a crumpled envelope. "I'm very sorry Doctor. Mr. Baker said to give you this note when I met you in Lagos. I forgot. I be very sorry." He smiled so engagingly and looked so genuinely sorry that Cecilia forgave him on the spot. Besides, it meant that Tim had thought of her.

She walked up the shallow steps and followed Sunday into a large, pleasant and deliciously cool interior. Sunday made straight for a small desk behind which sat a pretty girl, a couple of telephones in front of her.

"Doctor Onochie," he said to the girl. "New member of staff." With that he smiled at Cecilia. "She will look after you, Doctor," he said, and was gone before Cecilia had time to say goodbye, let alone give him a little something for himself.

Standing at the desk she ripped open Tim's note. Finding that she was to ring him on his extension number, she asked the girl to get it for her at once.

"You will be staying here for a few days, Doctor Onochie, until your flat is ready. Would you care to go to your room and take the call there?" Cecilia smiled at the girl but shook her head. She couldn't wait to hear Tim's voice.

It only took a second and then she could hear him on the other end of the line and she felt warm and secure, her disappointment at the airport forgotten.

"Hello, Cecilia love, welcome to RCA. Did you have a good trip?" His voice sounded calm but happy, just as she had remembered it. When she was with him she felt like a ship sheltering in port, safe from the stormy seas outside.

"Oh, darling, I can't tell you how good it is to hear your voice, and yes, I did have a good trip, or rather would have had, except that it was my bad luck to attract the plane pest. But never mind about him, I'm here." Cecilia's eyes were shining, her face, softened by love, was breathtakingly attractive. She might not be a classic beauty, but she was a beauty all the same.

"Look, can you hang on for a few minutes? Order a coffee or something cool, I'll be with you in about fifteen minutes. There's so much I want to bring you up about," Tim said, and Cecilia thought she detected a note of caution in that voice she knew so well it was almost a part of her.

"All right, Tim, don't worry about me. I think I'll get settled in my room and. . . ." But she was interrupted hurriedly by Tim.

"No, don't do that darling. Wait until I see you. I'll try to make it in ten minutes, then we have the rest of the morning to ourselves."

"Very well love." Cecilia was so happy at the thought of seeing Tim again that she would have agreed to anything.

Putting the receiver down, she thanked the girl, who directed her to the little snack bar where she could get a drink. Leaving her luggage at the desk, she slung her bag over her shoulder and made for the snack bar. It was very clean and had a panoramic view of the surrounding countryside to the hills in the distance.

Having got her drink and fallen for a very American looking hot dog – Cecilia did not have a moments worry about her waistline and breakfast had been at five thirty – she sauntered out on to the wide, gleaming white polished terrazzo verandah, and sat at one of the little tables provided. It was

32

very pleasant, well sheltered by the wide overhang and with a cooling breeze to take away the stifling heat. She looked at the view. It was so beautiful that she felt tell-tale tears stinging behind her eyes. Close at hand on the right, there was the pool then a bank of assorted bougainvilleas, their peach, pinks and purples a riot of colour. Then she could see a little below them, before the hill sank into the valley, tennis and badminton courts. Beyond, she looked across the tops of palms, irokos and casurinas, to the rocky mountains beyond, where she could just see the signs of quarrying.

She sighed contentedly, she was very sensitive to beauty. In the lab it was efficiency that mattered, but a well kept lab had a kind of functional beauty too.

After refreshing her lipstick, which she used very lightly, she ran her fingers through her curls, to try to tidy them, and settled to wait for Tim, all fatigue forgotten in the excitement of the moment. Besides, who could feel fatigued looking at such a beautiful view, bathed in brilliant sunshine.

Cecilia didn't have long to wait before she caught a glimpse of Tim's familiar figure coming along the terrace towards her. She rose to her feet and sped like a gazelle to meet him. They put their arms round each other and Tim gave her a smacking kiss on the lips. Dear reliable Tim, Cecilia thought, looking up into his tanned face. His already blonde hair had been streaked almost white by the sun and even his neat little moustache was lighter, she noticed.

Arms linked, they walked to the table where she had left her bag.

"You are looking gorgeous, my sweet, just as I remembered you," Tim said, giving her hand an affectionate squeeze. "And you look exactly as I saw you in my dreams, only a lot browner. You re catching up with me," Cecilia replied, smiling radiantly at him.

"Pick up your bag, darling," he said, "I am taking you to my little pad, so that we can be alone together. I don't want to have to share you with anybody. Thank heavens the boss is away. He would not have approved of me taking time off to greet my fiancée."

"You make him sound a real slave driver. Surely you are senior enough to be trusted to do the job properly," Cecilia asked, her voice sharp with censure.

"Considering that the lowest form of life here are the Ph.D students, you would think that most of us were responsible about our jobs, wouldn t you? The trouble is," he continued, as he reclaimed her heavy cases from the desk and started walking towards the exit, "he is a fanatic about his research programme. Most of the scientists are enthusiastic or they wouldn't be here, but he lives, eats and sleeps it."

"Is he married?" Cecilia asked as she opened

the door for him.

"Thanks," Tim manouvred the cases through the doorway. "No, that's one of his problems. No serious woman friends either that I can see. Women are strictly for play and not to be taken seriously at all."

"What does he look like?" Cecilia asked, as he stowed her luggage away in the boot.

"Oh, I suppose you'd call him good looking, if you like that sort. Rather obvious I think.' He slammed the boot shut. "The women fall for him, not that he seems to notice."

"Do I detect a slight note of envy?'' Cecilia teased, as she seated herself beside him. Tim looked annoyed, an angry flush staining his cheeks. "Certainly not," he replied, shortly.

She bent to kiss his cheek, placatingly, inwardly chiding herself for her lack of tact. She had forgotten that Tim had no sense of humour with regard to himself. He took himself very seriously, and it was one of the qualities that she admired in him. "Hey!" she exclaimed suddenly, "we were talking so intently about our boss that I didn't think. You were a chump lugging my bags to the car, when I am to stay at the hostel for a few days."

"Never mind," he answered, lightly, "I can always take them back."

They were driving between elegant houses whose well kept open plan gardens edged the road on either side.

"These are lovely inside, Cecilia. I don't live in one of course. Not yet. I have a flat in that block over there. Just two rooms, kitchen and bath, but they are nice enough and it has a lovely view over the lake. We get all our water from there. And by the way, it's quite safe to drink straight from the taps."

"No boiling?" She couldn't quite believe it.

"No boiling. The water is treated at a central plant. We have central airconditioning too. '

"No wonder they can get the cream of the scientific world to come here," Cecilia said. "It's a dream world."

"Yes and very international, but all the same a little ghetto-ish. With such good facilities on Campus, people tend not to mix with the outside world, and that means we live in each other's pockets. It's as if there is a searchlight on you sometimes: your slightest action is noted," Tim warned.

"I can imagine," Cecilia answered. "But that won't apply to us. I can't wait to take you to meet my family and they are dying to meet you."

"Can't do that yet, I'm afraid," he answered almost too quickly. "Too much work at the moment."

"Oh, what a pity. They'll be so disappointed. And they haven't seen me for so long. But they'll understand, don't worry. When I ring them later this afternoon I'll tell them not to expect us yet awhile. "Cecilia could not keep the disappointment out of her voice, but made a determined effort, and changed the subject. "Well if the work facilities are anything like the living facilities. . . ."

"They are, darling. I can't wait to show them to you."

As he was speaking, Tim drew up outside a modern block of flats. "Here we are, darling — home."

"Will I have a flat here too?" Cecilia asked, getting out of the car and feeling the hot sun burning her back. It was a pleasant sensation after cold England.

"Wait and see," Tim parried teasingly, as taking her arm he led her into the cool shade of the entrance hall. "I'm on the first floor, that's what gives me such a nice view." Outside the door of his flat Tim stopped, and drawing her to him, kissed her gently on the mouth, "Welcome home, my love," he said, softly.

For a moment Cecilia had the memory of other lips, more demanding ones, that had recently kissed her. The feeling Tim's lips invoked was quite different; safe and warm and loving.

"I feel like carrying you over the doorstep — old English custom," Tim said, reaching to pick her up in his arms. He wasn't much taller than she, but he was strongly built and could have carried her slender body with ease.

"No!" Cecilia said sharply, pulling away from him, "That's for brides isn't it? Not until we're married. It might bring us bad luck." Tim ignored her, and picking her protesting body up in his arms he strode through the open door. As he placed her on her feet inside the hallway he drew her close, whispering, "What's the difference, we soon will be."

Tim was right. They would be married soon anyway wouldn't they? She returned his kiss, then running her hand through his straight blonde hair, she said, "You must think me a silly old-fashioned girl. It's just that I want everything to be perfect on the day." Her eyes pleaded with his for understanding, but she was puzzled by his expression. Then he smiled, put his arm round her waist and led her into the sitting-room. She gave a gasp of delight.

"I thought you'd like it, sweetheart," Tim said, beaming with pleasure. "Have you ever seen such a romantic love nest?"

At the words "love nest", Cecilia stiffened, but her pleasure in the room soon over-rode her uneasiness. It was a fairly large room with ceiling to floor glass doors on to the balcony. The floor was black and white terrazzo, with gay scatter rugs in a brilliant burnt orange, tan, and purple pattern. The furniture, consisting of two lounge chairs and a three seater sofa, was in tan cow-hide. They had scatter cushions in pale lemon and lilac. They were arranged to face the balcony with a beautiful view of the lake. There was a coffee table in smokey grey glass and the dining table, across the room by a smaller side window, was of the same smokey glass. The dining chairs were upholstered in tan velvet. And there were lush plants everywhere. Some trained up the walls and others in large earthenware pots on stands, whose leaves trailed prettily down to the floor.

"It's lovely, Tim, really lovely. Just fancy! I thought we'd have very utilitarian accommodation."

"I was incredibly lucky. A Scandanavian bloke lived here before me. Been here for some time, so he was allowed furniture of his choice. When he was leaving he didn't want it shipped home, so I grabbed it." He looked very pleased with himself, as he led Cecilia to see the rest of the flat. "I'll give you the guided tour and then let you freshen up before I feed you," he said, as he held open another door that led out of the arched hallway.

This was the bedroom. It too was large, but a little too masculine for Cecilia's taste. There was a comfortable looking double bed in the centre of one wall, the wooden headboard and bedside tables being an integral part of it, and there were a couple of very functional bedside lamps. The dressing table, in matching wood with the headboard and the chest of drawers, was business-like and rather spartan. Over in the far corner of the room, in a separate alcove with its own window, stood a desk, covered with books and papers and there was a bookcase on the wall beside it. The rug and the bedspread relieved the stark masculinity of the room a little, the former being fluffy and in a gay red, while the latter was in a deep purple and red pattern.

"It's very nice for you, but a little stark for my taste. Definitely a man's room," Cecilia said, with a smile, as she turned to walk out.

"That can always be altered, but it has a nice large bed, hasn't it?"

Cecilia could no longer deny her uneasiness. "What are you getting at, Tim?" she asked quietly, once they were back in the lounge to which she had determinedly led them. Tim pulled her into his arms, "Darling, this isn't the time to say this. I had planned to make my proposal after lunch, but you have asked, so here goes." He led her over to the settee and when they were seated took both her hands in his saying, "It occured to me, that even an old-fashioned girl like you might agree to share my bed and board," and as he felt her stiffen, added hurriedly, "seeing as how we are planning to get married soon."

"Oh, Tim! I thought you understood. Much as I love you, in fact because I do love you, I don't want to jump the gun. I want our wedding night to be a proper wedding night. And I don't want to be like so many other girls and go pregant to the altar." She looked pleadingly into his eyes, continuing, "You've been so good and understanding up until now. Please don't spoil it."

Tim rose abruptly to his feet, "I'm glad you realise it. In this day and age! A liberated woman too — in every other way — but not taking the pill and hanging on to her virginity as if it mattered more to her than anything else on earth. Certainly more than her fiance."

"Please, please don't be angry with me," she pleaded, her heart in her eyes.

"And just what sort of a fool shall I look to everyone here? This is a sophisticated society, Cecilia, not something out of the ark."

His hard, angry tone bit into her soul, but she was fighting for something that she believed in with all her heart. "I'm sorry, but I don't agree that to be modern you have to sleep around."

"I should hardly call living with your fiancé, sleeping around," Tim replied bitingly, "and besides, you've told me that most of your Nigerian men demand it nowadays."

They were nearer a quarrel than they had ever been before and it cut Cecilia to the quick. Gone was the lovely joyous feeling that she had had. Ignoring his remark by deliberately not rising to it, she tried a new tack. "Anyway darling, do be practical. We could hardly both work in one room and at only one desk," she said with a lightness she was far from feeling.

"And that's another thing. Why did you have to go and rush things? Why did you apply for a job out here so soon after I had one?" Tim sat down sulkily on the edge of the settee, looking for all the world like a small child. Cecilia looked up at him, her eyes big bruised pools of pain. Never before in their relationship had Tim underlined that they came from different cultures. They had never found it to be a barrier.

She was aghast. Tim didn't want her at RCA?

"I thought you'd be pleased that we should be working together and that I managed to land a job here entirely on my own merit, without your help or anyone elses. I told you in my letter I never even mentioned that I was engaged to you."

"Yes, and just where do you think that leaves me! My fiancee applies for a job here and I don't even know about it." He stood up angrily and lit a cigarette.

Cecilia looked at him, deflated. She had meant everything for the best and Tim was angry with her, angry as he had never been before.

"I've only been here six months. Not long enough to establish myself," he continued, throwing the used match in an ash-tray. "I wanted to bring you out as my fiancee and then get you a job. That's what I'd planned to do, when I was settled."

Cecilia sat down on the sofa. "So I was to be given a job as a favour to you, was I? Why didn't you let me in on your plans for my professional future?" She was bitterly hurt by his attack on her, but she was angry too. She was proud of her professional reputation. Tim knew that, and just how much it meant to her.

"I could say the same to you, couldn't I?" Tim

said, grinding his hardly smoked cigarette out in the ash-tray.

He was right, but she had only kept it from him in case she hadn't got the appointment. And she thought he would have been so pleased! Her anger went as quickly as it had come, as she looked up at Tim. "We're quarrelling. For the first time we are quarrelling." She was torn apart, and now the effects of the tiring journey of thousands of miles, hit her. She felt washed out, jaded and unhappy. She had imagined it all so differently: she had pictured them laughing and happy, each as pleased as the other to be together again.

Tim saw the tired look on her face, the unhappiness in her eyes, and his conscience smote him. He had been too hasty, and stung by her refusal to shack up with him, he had said more than he intended. He rose and crossed to her, and sitting down beside her, he took her into his arms. "What an unfeeling beast I've been. Can you ever forgive me? And on your first day too." He wiped away the tears which she could no longer hold back. "Come. What you need is some food and then a rest. After that we can talk."

"And see the campus?" Cecilia asked, a watery smile breaking through her tears.

"I promise, darling." Tim kissed her gently on the mouth.

The pleasant lunch that Tim gave her, followed by a rest in the cool of her room at the hostel, did much to restore both Cecilia's body and her spirits. If she had any lingering doubts, she had put them firmly out of her mind by the time Tim came to pick her up to show her over the campus.

First they had started with a ride round the grounds: beside the lovely reservoir with its many exotic birds, to the experimental fields on the outer rim of the campus and then through the residential areas. They even paid a visit to the little school house. He had kept to the last the places that he knew would interest her the most — the hot houses and the labs where the experiments were carried out. These were in the same area as the office and administration blocks. He parked his car in the space provided, and they had walked up the hot outside staircase from the car park, to pass through a swing door which opened on to a long, cool corridor. This had lots of doors with names on leading off it.

Tim had taken her first to his office, furnished with a plain desk, and with plenty of bookshelves. He had mentioned casually that he did most of his work there, staying on after the office staff left in the afternoon.

Then he had shown her to her office. Her name was already on the door, and this gave Cecilia a great thrill. Her office was the exact replica of Tim's, except that it looked very empty — no books on the shelves or papers littering the desk. Tim had then pointed out the Group Director's office and had taken her into the outer office, to introduce Obi's Secretary, an attractive, efficient young woman. He asked her when the Director was expected back and was told that they expected him back the next day.

Later, sitting out on Tim's balcony, a glass of cold, fresh mango juice in her hand, watching the wonderful pinks and purples of the setting sun dye the lake to the most beautiful rich wash of colour, Cecilia's thoughts were of the wonderful labs that she had seen that day. Being an international institution, RCA got funds from all over the world, and it showed in the equipment. Cecilia was simply longing to get to work. The incubators that she would be using to breed millions of parasitoids, were as up to date as any she had seen abroad. And everyone that she had met who was working on the project seemed as keen as she was.

Theirs was but a small portion of the work going on, she realised that. There were many other programmes: to enrich the protein content of rice and other starches and cow peas too: to alter the genetics so that bigger and hardier plants would be produced: to make the various tubers, roots, and grasses, pest resistant — very neccessary in tropical countries where pests were so multitudinous.

Inspite of this, she could not help feeling that for the Third World, her own project was one of the most meaningful. If by Biological Control they could rid maize and cassava of the pests that preyed on them, they would be a long way towards staving off the famine that now threatened countries whose people ate maize and cassava as their staple food. Cecilia cared, cared very much for people, and especially for her own countrymen and women. It was her driving ambition to help prevent that. famine.

"Penny for them?" Tim interrupted her reverie, as coming back from freshening up his drink, he sat on the wicker chair beside her.

"I was thinking about what I saw today."

Cecilia had no idea how attractive she looked in the cool, mint-green, sleeveless dress she had changed into. The flaming colour of the sky giving her lovely skin a warm hue. And to top it all, dazzling lights shone out of her eyes, seeming to light up the darkening scene.

"Darling," Tim murmured huskily, as putting his drink down, he reached for her. She melted into his arms and their lips met. "I can't tell you how sorry I am about this morning, I. . . ."

Cecilia put a finger to the lips that had just kissed hers so tenderly, "Not another word. I have already forgotten about it," she smiled into his light grey eyes.

"Good," Tim said, "because this will be a convenient time to get you up on the set-up here." He took a long drink of his whiskey soda. "One needs to tread carefully, if one wants to get on. It is absolutely essential that your Group Director

.likes you, for. . ."

"Surely not," Cecilia interrupted, "So long as your work is good what do personalities matter?" She was shocked to think anything different.

"You'll find out, " Tim said, a small frown of annoyance darkening his features, "so I want you to go all out to charm Obi, darling, for both our sakes." Tim smiled entreatingly at her. "You could charm the birds off the trees."

"But I thought this Obi was impervious to feminine charms," Cecilia said picking up her glass again. "Anyway, I thoroughly disapprove of using any feminine charms I may or may not possess, at work. It's unscientific and he would have every right to despise me for it." She took a sip of her drink, "I'm sorry darling, but. . ."

"Not even for me?" Tim begged. "After all I am being very nice to the provost's daughter." He stopped suddenly, looking a little sheepish, and then continued hurriedly. "Nothing you need to worry about, darling, nothing serious you know, just a little light flirtation." He felt Cecilia's gaze on him. Well poor kid, she is bored out here, not many people of her own age about. There was a little defiance in his glance now, as he defended himself. "We can't all be paragons of virtue like you," he added, a bitter note in his voice.

Cecilia was immediately contrite, poor Tim. Her refusal to sleep with him before marriage was very hard for him to accept in this day and age. "Darling," she was anxious that they shouldn't have another quarrel, she couldn't bear it, "I trust you, and I'm sure that you wouldn't use the daughter of the Provost to work out your frustrations on." Tim looked at her sharply, but could detect no malice in her face. "As to my making up to our boss – I can't do as you wish, but I am good at my job, so let's hope that that will suffice."

Tim gave in with rather bad grace, "I might have known. Silly to ask you really. I just hoped that you would co-operate, as my whole career is at stake." He bit his bottom lip.

"Mine too, or have you forgotten?" Cecilia asked quietly.

"No, of course I hadn't, but after all my career has to be more important than yours, darling. You are the one who has to have the babies and. . ."

"Do the housework," Cecilia finished his sentence. "Is that what you were about to say, Tim?"

"Of course not, darling," Tim sounded injured, "I'm not a male chauvinist, you know that. But I do think that in a marriage one of the partners has to be the dominant one."

The fast approaching night, hid the hurt in her eyes, as she answered, "I have always considered marriage should be an equal partnership."

"And so do I darling. Never fear, I shall be the most considerate of husbands." He rose to his feet, "Time to go in and eat. Enough talk of work," and he drew her to her feet, holding her close. He kissed her lips and his hand caressed the rounded curve of her breast to harden the nipples. But Cecilia's body failed to respond, her mind was too troubled.

As if sensing that he had gone too far, Tim was charm itself during the rest of the evening, and she gradually relaxed and began to feel safe again. This was the Tim that she knew, that she loved, not the one that she had had her first glimpse of earlier in the day.

And he really had gone out of his way to please her. He had laid on another delightful meal, but this time a Nigerian one, to surprise her — a lovely hot pepper soup and yam.

"Tim," she exclaimed, "however did you cook such a delicious meal? You certainly kept your talents well hidden when we were together at the Imperial College. I had no idea that you knew how to cook African food." Tim smiled sheepishly. "I have a confession to make. I told Dolapo's wife that I wanted to feed you today and she took pity on me. She can cook any kind of food and all deliciously. She likes eating too!"

Cecilia burst out laughing, and getting up from the table she went to the back of Tim's chair, putting her arms round his neck and kissing his ear. "I love you for it, and you certainly had me fooled— and impressed."

"I'm glad you don't mind. I did so want to have you ·to myself our first evening together." He turned his head and pulled her towards him. "I've

49

missed you so, Cecilia.''

"And I've missed you too darling, so much.''

"And now it's as if we've never been apart." He kissed her nose, and then putting her firmly away from him, said, "Chores first, like in the old days," and rose to his feet.

Cecilia started to clear the table. "Does Dolapo's wife want the dishes back tonight?" she asked Tim, as he came to help her.

"No love. Nike will send her steward over in the morning. We don't even need to do the washing up."

"Oh, I couldn't possibly leave these dirty dishes around until morning. It won't take me a jiffy," and she started looking for an apron in the small but well planned kitchen.

"You won't find an apron. I'm afraid that on my own I take all my meals at the hostel." Tim put the wine glasses down carefully on the draining board while Cecilia ran the hot water. "Was Dolapo that nice shortish man working out in the field?" she asked, squirting the washing-up liquid into the basin and then beating it with her hand.

"That's right. He's in charge of Release and Follow-up, so you won't see much of him in the labs. By the way, I quite forgot. Nike is giving a small welcome party tomorrow night for you and a couple of other new folk. You'll like her. She's fun." Tim put the dishes that he had dried on a tray on the worktop. "Of course there will be a much bigger one later, given by the provost and his wife. It's a very social life out here as you'll see. The wives see to that, starting with the provost's wife down to the wife of the most junior scientist. They all do their bit to help to organise the social life of the campus."

"Much as I love parties, I hope they won't interfere with my work. I have articles and papers I want to write, and. . ."

"So have I too, my love," Tim put down the tea towel, "Is that all then?"

Cecilia cast a quick glance around. "I think so, yes." Tim heaved a sigh of relief, "Thank heavens. Now we can get down to more important things." He took her unresisting hand and led her out to the balcony, where an enormous full moon was shedding a mysterious silvery light over the lake and its banks. The air was moist and still, but throbbing with the shrill notes of a thousand cicadas.

Dear Tim, everything so thought out, so organised, Cecilia thought, before Tim's arms went round her and his lips found hers. It was much later when, having bid Tim goodnight, she started to make her preparations for bed. She had un-packed everything but her cabin bag earlier in the afternoon, so it was easy for Cecilia to find her simple cotton nightie with the demure frill of broderie anglaise round the low cut neck and hem. It was only when she was in the little bathroom that she remembered that her nail-brush was in the cabin bag. She hurried back into

51

the bedroom again to search for it. Much better just to tip everything out on the dressing table top, she thought to herself, when she had difficulty in finding it. Suiting actions to words she tipped it upside down. Out fell a couple of books, a handkerchief, her diary, her travelling make-up-cum-toilet bag and her purchases from the duty free shop. She looked again. There must be some mistake. She had only bought one eau de toilette, and she had already given Tim his after-shave, so what on earth was in that other box? It looked like perfume. The stewardess must have made a mistake.

Cecilia picked it up. It was a bottle of *Miss Dior* perfume. There was a card stuck through the plastic wrapping. She pulled it out and gave a little gasp as she read, "To Cecilia, to go with her toilet water and to remind her of me — wherever she is."

There was no signature, there didn't need to be one. Cecilia knew full well who was responsible for the bottle of perfume in her bag, and she was not amused. She still wasn't rid of Ezeilo after all — drat the man! She wished she could have the pleasure of returning his unwanted gift. Never mind, she would give it away instead. Mike should have it.

Chapter Three

Cecilia was up bright and early the next day, eager to settle in to her new office. She had a quick refreshing shower and then put on a pair of serviceable jeans and a plain apple green cotton top. Her one concession to femininity was the little gold cross hanging round her neck. She combed her curls adding some conditioning gel, smeared a hint of lipstick across her lips, then picking up her bag she sallied forth to breakfast.

Early as she was, she did not expect to meet Tim there, because he had told her last night that he had to leave at the crack of dawn to get to their experimental farm, seventy kilometres away. He couldn't avoid it, as Obi had told him to do a check there, before he came back.

Cecilia had turned down Tim's offer to take her with him, regretfully, for she would have loved to see how the experiments were going, but first, as she explained to him, she wanted to settle in and catch up on all the notes she would have to read in order to know what state the work that she would be taking over had reached by the time her predecessor left.

After a light breakfast of fruit juice, toast and coffee, Cecilia picked up her papers and the essential books that she had brought with her and walked across to the office block. She had no difficulty in finding it and thoroughly enjoyed the brief walk in the company of several cattle egrets, so comical on the ground but so beautiful on the wing. They seemed totally un-afraid of her, treating her with disdain, looking at her down their long yellow beaks. They looked so clean, with their snowy white feathers that it was hard to imagine them picking ticks from the backs of cattle, hence earning themselves the common name of tick birds.

On entering the building she made her way to the office of the Group Director's Secretary, who, Tim had told her had a set of keys for Cecilia, for her office and the various labs that had to be kept locked.

Work started early here, and although it was not yet eight o'clock, Ola was already there, taking the cover off her typewriter. She gave Cecilia a very warm smile.

"Good morning Doctor Onochie. I expect you would like your keys." She opened a locked drawer in her desk and taking out a bunch of keys handed them to Cecilia. "That large one is for your office and the others are all clearly marked."

"Thanks Miss. . . I'm afraid I don't know your name," Cecilia said, returning Ola's friendly smile with an equally friendly one of her own.

"Miss Akinola, but everyone calls me Ola. I hope you will do the same, doctor."

"Then you must call me, Cecilia."

"Right." Ola was agreeably surprised by Cecilia's friendliness. So many of the 'been-to's' felt themselves too superior to bother to be nice to a mere secretary. She beamed with pleasure, "Now is there anything you want to know? Anything I can help you with? I'm not too busy, with Doctor Obi away. I shall be busy from tomorrow though, he's a real slave-driver when he's around."

"So I've heard," Cecilia remarked dryly.

"But nobody minds, he works twice as hard as anyone else and never asks anything of others that he wouldn't do himself."

It was obvious that Ola really liked and respected her boss. Her voice was full of admiration.

"He sounds like a scientist after my own heart, ' remarked Cecilia. Ola's description of the Group Director was quite different from Tim's, but although Cecilia was longing to question the girl further about her boss, she did not believe in gossiping about colleagues behind their backs.

"And good looking with it." Ola looked down at the engagement ring sparkling on Cecilia's finger, "But I can see that won't interest you. '

"No, I'm engaged to Tim," Cecilia replied.

Ola looked surprised, "You don't mean Tim Baker?" she asked. Cecilia nodded. "Well he's a dark horse! Never mentioned a word about it." Ola looked amazed.

"No, well I'm not here as his fiancee, you know. I'm here to do my own work. Which reminds me. Where will I find the files my predecessor left? I want to spend today finding out about my job."

"I'll get them for you. They're in a cupboard in Doctor Obi's office." She rose from her desk. "Hang on a minute."

Watching her go into the inner office, Cecilia thought how pleasant she was and how smart she looked in her crisp, cream pleated skirt and matching shirt. She was wearing some gold of course. All women loved gold and Cecilia herself was no exception — in moderation. Ola's earrings were small and well suited to her tiny ears: a tiny diamond nestled in a ring of gold. Altogether she made a pleasing sight. As Ola came briskly back, Cecilia couldn't help wondering if Doctor Obi thought so too.

"Don't hesitate to come to me if you have any problems or queries, Cecilia," Ola said, as she handed a bulky pile of files over. "Scientists come and go, but I go on for ever," she added, grinning, as she sat down behind her typewriter.

"I bet you could run the Group single-handed," Cecilia said with a smile.

"Administratively, I bet I could too."

As Cecilia was walking to the door, Ola called after her. "If you feel like a coffee about ten thirty, come round. I don't expect you will have got yourself organised with a flask and instant coffee yet."

Cecilia turned at the doorway, "I can see we are going to get on very well Ola, and thanks, I will most certainly take you up on your offer."

But Cecilia was lost to the world in the files that Ola had given her, so she was very surprised when there was a knock on her door and it opened to show Ola standing there with a steaming cup of coffee.

"I know you scientists," Ola said, with a grin. "So Mohammed has come to the mountain." She handed the cup of coffee to Cecilia who stretched her aching neck. "Sorry, I was lost to the world, but what an exciting stage these experiments are at. I couldn't have come at a better time." Ola looked at her, her head on one side, "You really are interested aren't you?" she said.

Cecilia nodded, "The success of these experiments matters more than anything else in the world to me," she said. "It could mean the difference between life and death to thousands of people on this continent."

"Poor Tim," Ola said quietly, as she left the room. But Cecilia didn't hear her, for her head was buried in the files once more.

She worked solidly all morning only dimly registering the sound of the siren which told the whole campus that it was twelve noon and lunchtime. Cecilia did not stop for lunch however, and it was not until four o'clock that after glancing at the slim gold watch on her wrist, she reluctantly put the files down. She then realised that she felt very hungry, so she decided to lock up, and go back to the snack bar for a toasted cheese sandwich or another of those delicious hot dogs she had had the day before.

Tim had promised to pick Cecilia up for the party that evening, so she had no worries about how to find the house. She wanted to make a good impression on her colleagues and their wives, and so dressed with care. She didn't have a lot of choice, as she had used up quite a bit of her luggage allowance on her books. She was undecided whether to wear a smart cocktail trouser suit in pure silk crepe de chine, or a deceptively simple jade green jersey dress. The trouser suit was in peacock blue with a gold trim round the sleeveless top and down the side seams of the trousers. A gold kid belt finished off the ensemble.

The dress was less dramatic and in the end Cecilia judged it the more suitable for her first introduction to this cosmopolitan and academic society.

After a cold shower, she splashed her *Miss Dior* eau de toilette generously on her slender form before slipping into her off-the-shoulder bra and lacey briefs. Then she slid her dress over her head and shoulders and smoothing it down over her slim yet femininely rounded hips, she looked at herself critically in the long mirror.

The dress clung to her figure making her appear even taller and more willowy than she actually was. It's shoe-string shoulder straps had a pretty diamante trim and sparkled attractively against her fine skin. The jade green colour of the dress made her large brown eyes burn and shimmer in contrast.

Cecilia was totally without conceit. Looking at herself with a critical eye, she decided that she was correctly dressed for the coming party. She did not notice how alluring she looked, how male glances would be drawn to her, as moths to a flame. It was not a false modesty, but she had always cared much more about her inner soul than her outward appearance. She had enough pride in herself to want to look her best, not to let her outward appearance betray her inner being, but that was all. Besides, most of her waking hours were spent in pursuits of the intellect, not worrying about clothes and make-up.

She applied her usual light touch of lipstick, choosing a bright red to contrast with her green dress. She dusted her face lightly with powder and smeared a hint of gold eye shadow on her eyelids. After running a comb through her dancing curls, which she found no amount of brushing could tame into a severity more befitting to an up and coming young scientist, she wondered why she had ever fallen for the temptation of a Californian Curl. She picked up a small gold clutch bag and shutting the door carefully after her, made her way down to wait for Tim.

Cecilia loved the vastness of the lounge in the hostel and never found it dull sitting there, for most of the world passed through it daily. Why, even in their small group, Tim had told her, there was an American, an Indian and a Korean, the latter, he had told her was very difficult to understand, but with good humour and goodwill they managed to communicate successfully. And the Indian had a beautiful wife who was a great party giver and a super cook. Cecilia hoped to meet them all at Nike and Dolapo's tonight, and of course, the great Doctor Obi — she gave a little nervous shudder at the thought of meeting her boss about whom she had already had such conflicting reports. Only one thing was certain about him, thank goodness, he believed in work and wasn't the sort to make a pass at her.

Tim came striding in, looking a little untidy. Cecilia smiled. He always did look untidy. That was one of the first things that she had noticed about him, and it was oddly appealing, and gave him a sort of little boy look.

"Hello darling, I hope I haven't kept you waiting," he said, kissing her cheek, "but that dratted land-

rover broke down on the way back and I have only just got in. Come on, let's go, I'm dying for a drink."
He took her hand and hurried her out, down the steps and into his car. Cecilia felt irked that he had made no remark about her appearance, especially as he was the one who was so keen for her to make a good impression.

"You haven't said if you approve of my appearance," she said, as he put the car into gear and they moved off.

"If I hadn't I would have told you," was his reply.

Cecilia felt a small pain in the region of her heart, for a little encouragement would have been welcome when she was about to meet a lot of strange people who were to be her colleagues and neighbours for the next few years. Then she silently chided herself and a loving smile lifted the corners of her mouth. She had long known that Tim was not the flowery sort, not given to compliments at all. Their relationship was based on true frienship and that, she was sure, was a better base than romantic love. Hadn't she told that wretched man on the plane just that? But she didn't want to waste any thoughts on him! So she proceeded to tell Tim about her day's work.

In a matter of minutes Tim pulled up outside a house that was ablaze with lights both outside and in, for Cecilia could see that the garden was hung with pretty coloured lights strung from the trees.

It was a lovely night for an outdoor party as there was just a little breeze, the moon was full and the sky a mass of twinkling stars.

There was already quite a crowd of people on the lawn, their talk and laughter mixing with background music. Tim was looking round for their hosts, when a bright happy voice cried out, "Welcome you two, and especially to you Cecilia." It was a lovely warm welcome and put Cecilia at ease at once. She immediately felt drawn to the short plumpish young woman coming towards them. "Thank you, you must be Nike. I've heard a lot about you," Cecilia said, smiling warmly.

"Oh dear! What have you been saying about me, Tim?" Nike shook her head at Tim in playful reproof.

She was wearing a long cotton dress, with a Wild West look to it, as it was becomingly checked in pink and blue with an open shirt neck and a deep, feminine frill round its full hem. She was not a pretty girl, but had a homespun charm about her that was very appealing. Cecilia liked her warmth, and there was an openness about her that she liked too.

"I say, she's much too pretty for you, Tim," Nike teased, as linking an arm through one each of theirs, she drew them towards the other guests. "And are you quite sure she's one of you egg-head scientists? She looks much too pretty to have a brain in her head." Cecilia couldn't help laughing, but she felt ridiculously pleased.

"The bar is in the usual place Tim. You get yourself a drink while I introduce Cecilia to all the other guests." She gave Tim no chance to refuse, as dis-engaging her arm from his, she gave him a small but determined shove in the right direction. She turned back to Cecilia with a bubbling smile. "Can't have one of my guests of honour monopolised by her fiancé. Come on then, I'll throw you in at the deep end."

The fairy lights cast a very romantic light over the scene, making everyone look more glamorous than they did in the light of day. Cecilia was no exception, and the men were all too eager to make her acquaintance. Nike told Cecilia what group each scientist belonged to, and often exactly what his job was.

"How do you know so much?" Cecilia asked her when they stopped briefly to grab a cool fruit punch.

"It's easy really. All our husbands are totally wrapped up in this place, and we hardly move off the campus, so if we didn't take an interest in it as well, life would be a little dull. Although I'm lucky. Our families both come from Ilesha, so I do manage to see quite a bit of them, and have a lot of social life off campus."

After a while, when she had introduced Cecilia to almost everyone there, Nike left her with Doctor Shivra and her Korean colleague, and went off to

see to the barbeque. At first, Mrs Shivra, resplendent
in the most gorgeous sari that Cecilia had ever seen,
and shimmering with jewels, chatted with them
while the motherly plump Korean lady stood
smiling and nodding. Her English was as poor as
Mrs. Shivra's was fluent. But eventually the talk
turned to work, as Cecilia had hoped, work being
foremost in her mind at present. Then the two
ladies slipped away to join a group of ladies, and
Dolapo joined their group.

A little later, inspite of her interest in their
discussion as to how they could persuade the
quarantine officials to give their permission to
import the batch of about a hundred parasitoids,
which were awaiting despatch at the Commonwealth
Institute of Entomology in London, Cecilia felt
that perhaps she ought to circulate. But on looking
round, she saw that the party had broken up into
little groups of scientists talking earnestly, groups
of wives, and a group of teenagers. Her fears were
put at rest, as everyone seemed quite happy with
the situation, and she continued to take part in
the discussion. "I can see their point. They see the
the country being over-run with a new pest from
South America, and they have had trouble enough
with the old ones ruining their cassava crops. We
must convince them that these are hyper parasites
with a host specivity, in this case, the green spider
mites, and if they should manage to eat all the
green-spider mites up, they will die as they will eat

nothing else."

"I agree, But it is easier said than done," put in Doctor Shivra. "We shall have to send you down to see them, maybe you will be able to persuade them where your predecessor failed." He smiled at Cecilia, acknowledging her charm.

"Well I certainly hope so," Dolapo said, "because we plan to be releasing millions of them per day over a vast portion of this continent in a few months time."

"If we get the special plane," said the Korean.

"And if we get the money to build our special factory," added Doctor Shivra.

"And if I am successful with the mass breeding. But those excellent incubators should give me a good start," Cecilia said.

"They are fine, aren't they? The very latest." Butch, the American in the team was very enthusiastic.

The talk went on. Dolapo excused himself, regretfully, but he was responsible for carving the barbequed pork, now scenting the night air with appetising smells.

Cecilia had forgotten all about Tim, and suddenly remembering and wondering why he hadn't joined them, she searched the guests for him and eventually saw him in conversation with a very young and pretty blonde girl. The provost's daughter, she thought wryly. Tim obviously meant what he had said. He was after friends in high places. She looked more closely at the girl. She would not have been human if she had not done so. She seemed a nice little thing, but almost a child. Cecilia felt no pangs of jealously. She was just wondering if the provost and his wife were here too when she heard Nike's voice calling her, and made her way to where she was standing on the outskirts of the crowd.

"I've saved the best for the last, Cecilia," she said, as Cecilia joined her. "I want to introduce you to your boss. He's just coming now."

Cecilia, her eyes following Nike's glance, saw a tall dark man emerge from the shadows of the drive into the glow of the fairy lights.

"Welcome back," Nike's voice rang out gaily. "Come and meet your new member of staff. You are in for shock. She's beautiful, Ezeilo."

Cecilia froze. It couldn't be the Ezeilo she had travelled with! She forced herself to look up into the face of the man towering above her, but before she met his eyes, she knew from the scent that it was him.

If Nike had meant to surprise Ezeilo she had succeeded beyond her wildest dreams. The eyes that met Cecilia's were obviously as shocked as hers, and every bit as displeased. Nike looked from one to the other puzzled. This wasn't quite the reaction she had expected. She rushed to break the grim silence. "The Provost has certainly done you proud this time, Ezeilo — beauty as well as brains."

"That remains to be seen," he replied, inferring

from the tone of his voice that he didn't agree with her.

Cecilia could feel the blood rush to her face. He was insufferable! How dare he be so rude! And how dare he jump to conclusions as to her ability! Her eyes, large pools of reflected coloured lights, flashed, as she politely held out her hand to him, "Yes it does, doesn't it? How do you do, Doctor Obi?"

He took her hand and her body tingled. She drew her hand away sharply as if it had been burnt.

"My friends call me, Ezeilo," he said, a sardonic smile turning up one corner of his mouth and making him look more attractive than ever.

"Do they, Doctor Obi," she answered, as coolly as she could manage, with her whole body trembling with rage — and some other emotion that she could not diagnose. "Now if you will excuse me I must go and look for my fiancé."

"I shouldn't dream of keeping you from him," ne answered icily, and dismissively, then turning to Nike asked, "How are my favourite children?"

"They won't go to bed until you have said hello. I made the fatal mistake of letting on that you would be sure to be back for the party. But I thought you were to have been back yesterday?"

Ezeilo put his arm affectionately round her waist. "Didn't I tell you? I had some work to do in Lagos after I landed." They were already walking towards the house.

Cecilia, who had meant to be the first to leave, stood looking after their receding backs as if rooted to the spot. Any way she didn't really want to find Tim yet, not now. She needed time to get over the shock!

At last, she made her trembling limbs move, and had just reached the outskirts of the crowd when a steward passed her with a tray laden with glasses of Nike's delicious punch. Cecilia took one, another drink was just what she needed to help pull herself round! She took a deep drink and almost instantly felt better. But she still didn't feel like making polite conversation, so moving out of the lit up area of the garden she wandered away from the crowd to gather her emotions into some semblance of normality. The last thing that Tim would want would be for her to make a bad impression. She knew that. He had made it more than plain. Poor Tim, she thought as she wandered between the hibiscus bush and under the sweet smelling frangipani at the bottom of the garden. Tim wanted her to be nice to her boss. If he only knew that she was an anathema to Ezeilo, already tried and found wanting.

The injustice of it brought angry tears to her eyes. Her private life was her own affair. Besides the Provost hadn't asked her about her private life, only if she were quite free to take a job abroad. Doctor Obi should have interviewed her himself if he was so fussy. But of course he was too busy touring the world!

Cecilia knew that she wasn't being fair, as the Provost had explained that he liked the Group Directors to interview their own prospective staff whenever possible. Unfortunately Doctor Obi had a fund finding tour already planned, and as the need to replace her predecessor was urgent, he had agreed to do the interviewing for him. "Of course," the Provost had added with a smile, "the ultimate decision does lie with me, but mostly I abide by the Group Director's."

Cecilia's determined little chin went up. She'd show that conceited chauvinist just what stern stuff she was made of. She was beginning to feel much better. Almost light-headed, and she swung round energetically to return to the party, head held high, the light of battle in her eyes, a fiery being, even in the silver moonlight.

"Why the hurry?" asked a voice that she knew only too well, as firm hands stopped her from stumbling.

"How long have you been standing there right behind me? I nearly fell over you." Her voice was accusing as she struggled to free herself from Ezeilo's iron grip. His eyes glinted dangerously, as holding her even closer to him, he said, "Temper! Temper! Anyone would think that it was I who bumped into you not the other way round. You should be apologising to me."

"I should apologise to you!" she exclaimed. Her

inability to free herself from his grasp, together with his nearness was fanning her temper. "Let me go!"

"Not until you say you're sorry like my good little girl." He was still smiling, she could see his teeth flashing white in the moonlight, but there was a hidden implacable strength behind it that sent shivers of apprehension down her spine. But still she fought to free herself. His fingers now biting cruelly into the tender flesh of her slender arms. "How dare you be so patronising. I am not your good girl and never will be."

"Of course, I had forgotten. You are Tim's girl, aren't you? — for the moment."

Cecilia could have hit him. She struggled harder and felt tears of pain and frustration sting behind her eyes. He held her so easily, as if she were a little kitten, and remorselessly pulled her closer until their two bodies were melded into one and she could feel the hardness of his long lean thighs against her hips, and his massive chest crushing her soft breasts.

Even before he bent his head to kiss her she felt strange tremors running through her whole body which began to tremble like an aspen leaf. If he hadn't held her so fast she would have fallen. She tried to turn her head away when she realised that he intended to kiss her, but to no avail. His mouth came down on hers bruisingly, forcing her lips apart, his tongue hungrily plundering the honey within. With one arm now firmly round her waist, his other started to roam over her body, bringing with its caresses a sweet langour that Cecilia had never experienced before, and one that she was powerless to resist. Of its own volition her mouth started to return his kisses, her arms stole round his neck and her body pressed itself to his. He gave a small moan of pleasure and pushing the tiny strap off her shoulder, cupped her rounded breast in his hand. At once her nipple hardened and he brought his mouth down to tease it to further delights with his teeth and lips. Cecilia felt herself swooning, totally out of control, she moaned with pleasure, as lifting his head from her breast she kissed him with complete abandon. She could feel the roused male hardness of him now, and it was only when she felt his hand caressing her most intimately that the realisation of what they were doing hit her. With a cry of pure distress she struggled to push him away from her. "No! No!" she cried, and some quality in her voice stayed him, for although he still held her, he stopped caressing her. His mouth twisted in a cynical smile and looking tauntingly into her now striken eyes, he said, "And you say you're Tim's girl!"

That did it! A blinding rage consumed her like a forest fire, and she lashed out and hit him a stinging blow on the cheek. "You beast!" she cried, eyes flashing fire. "You did it on purpose. You made me forget myself. I am Tim's girl and we are going to be married."

"I didn't do it all, you know," Ezeilo answered softly. "It takes two to tango, as they say, and I didn't feel you backing down." The blood rushed to Cecilia's cheeks. "I hate you for trying to make me into the kind of girl that fits your views of women." She was now bitterly ashamed of herself.

Looking deeply into the hurt pools of her large brown eyes, his own were strangely tender, as he said softly, "I don't think you do." Her eyes were held compellingly for a moment by his, and then he was gone. Oddly it felt to Cecilia that the moon had passed behind a cloud and she shivered.

She had no idea how long she had now been away from the party, but she knew she must get back. With a super human effort she pulled herself together, her thoughts once more in control, as she hurriedly tidied her hair as well as she could and pulled the glittering shoulder strap up over her shoulder, shame sending the blood again to her cheeks as she did so. How she loathed her new boss! But now she was even more determined to prove to him that she was as good a scientist as any man — in fact than most, as she knew to be true.

So it was with a brave smile on her lips and courage in her heart that she made her way back to the party.

No sooner had she appeared than Tim bore down on her. "Where have you been?" he asked irritably, "I've been looking everywhere for you. Doctor Wagner wants you to meet his wife." He took her arm and hurried her across the garden to where the provost was standing under a tall silk cotton tree. Doctor Wagner had a pleasant faced, plump woman by his side.

"Good, you've found her Baker." Doctor Wagner turned to his wife, "This is the young lady I was telling you about, my dear," he turned to Cecilia, "Doctor Onochie, meet my wife."

"I'm sure pleased to meet with you, Doctor Onochie." Mrs Wagner held out her hand, while smiling pleasantly at the younger woman. She had a delightfully warm personality and Cecilia took to her at once.

"And this is our daughter, Merribel. Mrs Wagner put her hand on the arm of the girl who was just passing. Cecilia held out her hand to the other girl in a friendly fashion, and Merribel took it hesitantly. Her face was no longer radiant as it had been when Cecilia had seen her talking to Tim earlier on. Now it was cloudy and Cecilia could see tears glinting in the baby blue eyes, as with a muttered, "Hello," followed by an even more mumbled, "Excuse me," Merribel hurriedly turned away, making for the house.

"You must forgive our daughter, Doctor Onochie," Mrs Wagner apologised. "She is very much in awe of you clever scientists. I hear you are engaged to Doctor Baker. Quite a surprise." She looked keenly at Tim. "We had no idea you were engaged, Doctor Baker." She had changed the subject from Merribel, but Cecilia had a shrewd feeling that she hadn't at all.

Tim looked embarrassed, "I had no idea that Cecilia would get a job out here so soon, Mrs Wagner. I thought it would be time enough to inform you when I had got her a job."

"But she surprised you by getting one for herself." Doctor Wagner gave Tim one of the penetrating stares that he was so famous for on the campus.

Cecilia could sense the undertones of the conversation. The Wagners were no fools. Hadn't Tim already told her that he had been entertaining their daughter? At once she flew to Tim's defence. "I was very naughty, Doctor Wagner. I do hope you will forgive me. I'm afraid I kept Tim quite in the dark. I never even told him that I knew there was a vacancy here, let alone that I had applied for the job. Poor Tim didn't expect me to come out for ages and ages, so no wonder he didn't tell anyone about me." She had done her best, but it seemed that Tim had almost over-played his hand with the Wagners.

"And you were very reticent with me, my dear. Not a mention that I already had your fiancé working here." It was Cecilia's turn to get one of the famous looks.

"I do hope you don't hold it against me, Doctor. It was very important to me, as a woman, to be sure that I got the job on merit alone."

"And you did, I assure you, my dear." Doctor Wagner smiled down at her, and she was looking devastatingly attractive. The emotion that Ezeilo had roused in her had left her glowing, and although her mouth was slightly swollen, she looked very soft and feminine and her eyes, enormous in her gamine face, shimmered from past excitement. She really was aflame. Doctor Wagner's heart felt warmed by her youth and beauty, as much as his intellect had been stimulated by her mind when he had interviewed her.

"I hope you will come and have tea with me one afternoon, my dear," Mrs Wagner invited Cecilia warmly.

"I'd love to, but I'm afraid we scientists don't stop for tea," Cecilia answered, rather ruefully.

"How stupid of me. Of course. Then perhaps you could come for a pre-dinner drink."

"I'm sure Cecilia could manage one of the all-girls-together-teas of yours that are so famous among the wives," Tim said ingratiatingly, with a quick warning glance at Cecilia.

"I'm afraid I really don't know about that, Not until I have learnt the routine of the place. Our Group Director might not approve, Tim," Cecilia said pleasantly but firmly. She was darn sure that Doctor Ezeilo Obi would not approve. Neither did she to be honest.

"That's quite all right, I quite understand. You

must be very dedicated to your research or Walter would not have engaged you." Mrs Wagner obviously did understand. Cecilia gave a little sigh of relief.

"Well, my dear, I think we must leave these good young people and circulate." Doctor Wagner smiled at Cecilia and Tim. "One of the penalties of the post." He shrugged his shoulders wryly, as he took his wife by the arm and they started to move away.

Cecilia had seldom seen someone on whom his position sat so pleasantly as Doctor Wagner. He hadn't a conceited or pompous bone in his body, top scientist and administrator though he was. She was most impressed by him, and could well see why he had been appointed. Of course she would have liked to see one of her own countrymen in the post, but that could well happen soon as no one held it for more than five years.

She liked Mrs Wagner too. She heaved another little sigh of relief: at least Tim could have no fault to find with her over them, for she would find it very easy to be nice to such a pleasant couple as the Wagners. Their Group Director, however, was another matter!

76

Chapter Four

When Cecilia and Tim said their 'goodbyes' and 'thank yous' and left the party it was still a night made for lovers. The whole campus was bathed in moonlight; it shimmered on the surface of the lake; it lent the blossoms on the trees and bushes, so vivid in the day, an ethereal, mystical quality. It was a velvety mysterious night and the shrill noise of the cicadas only made it more romantic.

But neither Cecilia nor Tim were in a romantic mood. Cecilia's nerves were stretched to breaking point. The episode with Ezeilo had shaken her to the core of her being, and on top of that she had been in an agony of mind lest she should have to encounter him again in front of Tim. She needed time to come to terms with the situation before that happened. At least she had been spared that tonight, she thought gratefully, as they walked to their car.

Tim on his part seemed wrapped up in his

thoughts and was unusually silent as he drove Cecilia back to the hostel.

Cecilia knew that she would have to break the news to him, that far from being able to further his career with their Group Director, in all probability she would blight it — if things here were as Tim said they were. She was hesitant to tell him. In the old days she would not have hesitated, sure that Tim would care as little as she would, but now she was not so sure. He had changed. She wondered bitterly, if she too hadn't changed, judging by her behaviour earlier on. Her generous mouth tightened into a thin line, as she thought of Ezeilo. How she detested his sort! She feared that she would find him impossible to work with, whatever Ola had said.

The noise of the handbrake brought her out of her reverie, followed by Tim's voice saying rather stiffly, "I want to come in to talk to you, so I've parked the car. The park is so close to the building you won't mind walking, will you?"

"Of course I won't," Cecilia replied, trying to make her voice light and cheerful. "Back in the UK we would have walked all the way to the party. It wasn't very far." She opened her door saying as she slipped out, "I have something to tell you too." She shut the door of the car carefully behind her. Tim hated people to bang the doors of his car. Then she walked round to his side and linked her arm through his. "Well, were you pleased with me, darling?" she asked lightly, as they passed a lovely white camelia bush, covered in ghostly blossoms giving off a heady perfume.

"If you want the truth, Cecilia, the answer is, no. That is what I want to speak to you about." Tim had stopped walking as he spoke.

Cecilia too stopped dead in her tracks. She felt shocked! This couldn't be Tim speaking to her in this schoolmasterish, disapproving voice. She slid her arm out of his, Her head tilting back in an instinctive defiant gesture to hide the hurt that his words had caused her.

"What on earth have you stopped for?" Tim asked, irritably, completely ignoring the fact that he was the first to stop. "We can't talk here. What has happened to you?" He took her arm and started to propel her towards the building. "You used to be so sensible."

For a moment it seemed as if Cecilia would resist, but then she relaxed and went with him up the steps and through the big swing doors into the cool interior, where they sat down in the now deserted lounge. There was a pause, then Cecilia spoke, in a voice she hardly recognised as her own. It was so coldly angry. "In what did I err? Was my dress wrong? Was I rude to anyone?"

"There's no need to lose your temper, Cecilia. Tim's voice was surly. "It isn't like you. I have always thought you the most reasonable of people, with such control of your emotions. It s one of the attributes I most admired in you."

"You have never before given me reason to lose that control, Tim. But you are right, I have always prided myself on it. I'm sorry." She got a grip on herself. "Please tell me what you think I did wrong tonight."

"I thought I had made it plain that I wanted you to behave more like my fiancé than a scientist, instead you insulted all the women there by spending most of your time talking shop with their men. Then, to top it all, when I wanted you I couldn't find you."

Cecilia was once more sitting bolt upright in her chair, her eyes wide open with astonishment, "Do you really believe that the women were insulted? I never intended that, Tim, it was just so natural to me to talk shop with my fellow scientists."

"And then you had to turn down Mrs Wagner's invitation to tea. Couldn't you even accept that to please me? I had told you how important it was that the Wagners should like you." Tim took a packet of cigarettes out of his pocket and lit one.

"But Mrs Wagner made it quite plain that she understood perfectly. As for the other women, it was they who moved away and formed little close knit groups of their own. I think you're being ridiculous. I shall ring Nike tomorrow and ask her." She was beginning to feel angry now.

"I suppose you bothered to make a point of meeting our Group Director too." Tim went on sarcastically, "Oh no! You were nowhere to be found when he made his appearance."

"As it happens, Nike introduced me to him, almost before he set foot in the place." She was sorely tempted to tell him how his precious Doctor Obi had treated her.

"I suppose you quarrelled with him." Tim was wallowing in such gloom that it suddenly occurred to Cecilia that he might have had a drop too much to drink. The punch had been very potent, as she well knew! Well, drunk or sober he might as well hear that much of the truth — it would help to prepare him for when she told him the worst. "As a matter of fact, yes."

Tim put his head in his hands, "I don't know what has come over you, Cecilia. You are like another person."

"And so are you, Tim. I never thought you could behave so childishly." Cecilia's eyes were full of scorn, but for all that, tears glinted on her dark lashes. Never in her wildest dreams had she thought that she and Tim could ever quarrel like this. She felt as if she were a child again listening to her parents exchanging angry words. She couldn't bear it a moment longer. Her tender heart was full of anguish, as she flung her arms around Tim's neck crying, "Darling! Darling! Please lets not quarrel. I came here so full of happiness at the thought that once more we should be working together, and preparing for our marriage, home in my own country, and now. . ." The unaccustomed tears threatened to choke her, and Tim could feel her

81

firm young breasts heaving up and down against his chest. This was a side of her that she had never shown him before and he did not quite know how to cope with it. She had always been so controlled and reasonable.

Cecilia's emotions were in a turmoil and her experience with Ezeilo in the garden had much to answer for. It was a long time since she had been a captive of her feelings and she struggled to gain composure, as Tim patted her on the back awkwardly, saying, "I'm sorry if I upset you, but I was upset. I felt so let down." He stubbed his cigarette out in the ashtray on the marble occasional table beside him, then putting his arm round her and holding her to his chest, continued, "You see darling, I really did have everything planned. I know we wouldn't have been together so soon, but you would have come here as my wife first, free to cope with the all-important social side. Then it would have been fine for me to get you a job. It would have looked right, do you understand?" He pushed her hair back from her forehead with a tender hand.

Truthfully, Cecilia could not follow his logic, but she decided that there had been enough hard words between them. "Is that why you never told me about the vacancy here, when it was right down my street?" He nodded.

"I had wondered about that." Cecilia had had every intention of asking him why, but now she knew the answer, and the answer to why he had never discussed his plans with her in his letters. He had planned their future as if she were to have no say in it. And her getting this job at this moment hadn't been in his scheme of things for their future. Their future or his future? A little voice whispered at the back of her mind, but she determinedly wouldn't listen to it, not tonight. She straightened up in his arms and taking his hands in her own, looked earnestly into his grey eyes with her tear-washed brown ones. "I'm sorry that you think I behaved badly tonight, just when I was thinking that I had been rather a success, too. I promise you to try harder in future, but I can never pretend that my job is of secondary importance to me, Tim, you know that. "He nodded.

"And I can never betray my ethical standards where that job is concerned, not even for you, so please don't ask me to, darling."

"As if I ever should," Tim said, kissing her gently on the mouth.

Much later lying awake in bed, Cecilia remembered her words and felt ashamed. Wasn't she being rather pompous about her ethical standards? She might stick to them over her work, but one obnoxiously conceited male had twice made her forget them where her personal relationship with Tim was concerned. Why did her treacherous body betray her by responding so violently to his caresses? When she had no trouble sticking to her moral

83

stand when Tim touched her?

The daylight was shining through the curtains before she fell into a troubled sleep.

Barely half an hour passed before her alarm went off and with a groan she staggered out of bed. Her head was throbbing badly, from a mixture of too much punch and too much emotion she diagnosed, as she hunted in her over-night bag for some panadol. Drat it! She felt as if a steam roller had run over her! This morning of all mornings, when their Group Director had called a meeting, and she would come face to face with him as her boss and taskmaster for the first time. She was not looking forward to it.

Cecilia recovered somewhat after a refreshing shower, and dressed carefully for her first official day on the job. She was glad that she would be armed with all the information in the file she had studied the previous day, and forewarned by her conversation on the plane, she knew what sort of woman her precious boss thought all female scientists were. She determined to look as little like an intellectual as she could, but never-the-less workman-like.

She chose a tight pair of jeans which as well as being workman-like, were also very feminine as they showed up every curve and emphasised her tiny waist. She wore them with a plain but figure hugging top in bright yellow, which left her slender young arms free. She made no attempt to flatten her curls, but fluffed them out becomingly round her fine-boned face. A little mascara to dramatise her large dark eyes and a touch of lipstick finished her toilet. She surveyed herself critically in the mirror. Yes, she would do, she decided. She would create the impression that she wanted to.

She was about to leave the room when she stopped, and turning back to the dressing-table she opened the bottle of perfume that she had meant to give away, and with a defiant toss of her head she applied it behind her ears. She'd show Doctor 'Clever' Obi that a woman could be feminine and a first class scientist as well!

Walking briskly through the heavy, damp mist of the early morning, Cecilia's spirits lifted and her energy returned. Work had always been a powerful stimulant to her and she was not going to let the meeting ahead dampen her enthusiasm. This morning, however, she did not notice the friendly tick birds around her feet. Her mind was busy with an experiment she wanted Doctor Obi's permission to get under way.

From the notes she had followed carefully, she knew experiments had been made when it was discovered that some of the exotic predators had not taken kindly to their new environment, thousands of miles away from their home in South America. Excellent though she considered those experiments to be, she had discovered that they left one factor out when observing the predator eggs in the petrie dishes. She had felt the elation that all scientists must feel when they know they have discovered a more precise way to observe an experiment, and so to make their findings conclusive. She was banking on her boss being detached enough not to let their personal antagonism blind him. She determined to bring it up that morning.

She glanced at the watch on her slim wrist. Ten minutes to go. Good, she would slip into her office first and pick up that file.

The meeting was being held in Doctor Obi's round table, on which Ola had already set a flask of water, glasses, ashtrays and a piece of paper in front of each seat, with the agenda. Cecilia gave Ola a friendly smile when they met in the outer office, and then walked in, head held high exuding a confidence that she did not feel. Now that the moment had come, she was extremely nervous and felt rather like a new girl at school. On entering, she found that she was not the first. Doctor Soon and Butch were already there. Butch gave her a breezy grin, saying, "Hi! Good party last night wasn't it? But that punch of Dolapo's! Have I got a head on me." Mr Soon bowed with great politeness, saying nothing. Before she could return their greetings Doctor Shivra and Dolapo appeared and greeted the others in a friendly fashion. What a nice bunch they seem, Cecilia thought. If only she could say the same of their Group Director!

She was already on first name terms with Butch and Dolapo, but she sensed an Eastern reserve about Doctor Soon and Doctor Shivra: she wasn't sure that she would ever be on first name terms with them. As for Doctor Obi — sometimes she thought of him as Doctor Obi and sometimes as Ezeilo. She found it rather muddling.

Voices broke into her reverie, they were saying, "Good morning, Ezeilo." Telling her that her mentor had arrived on the dot of eight, and also that his team all used his first name. She honestly did not know what she would call him.

As he brushed past her, once again she got a whiff of the scent of him, sending her mind racing back to their other meetings and sending her heart racing too, much to her annoyance. She sat down on a chair and took out her pen and notebook from her brief-case. Putting the brief-case down, she pulled the chair in to the table and sat back, looking cool and business like, but on glancing down at her hand that held the pen she was annoyed to see it trembling.

There was a general bustle as the others took their seats. It was only then that Cecilia realised that Tim was missing. She looked at her watch, it was a few minutes after eight. She felt unreasonably let down. He really should have been on time. Glancing at her boss she saw that he had noticed Tim's absence, as he pointedly glanced at the large wall clock. Then he looked up at the faces round the table, "As you can see from the agenda, I have called this meeting to report on my travels, which I am relieved to say were most successful. You may however bring up any matters arising, or urgent."

How capable and confident he looked, Cecilia couldn't help thinking, as she observed him through her lashes. And how powerful. Even across the table she could feel the strong masculine vibes emanating from him, and they disturbed her, as she took in the neatness of him: he too was in jeans, taut against his muscular thighs and slender hips. His crisp white cotton shirt was open at the neck exposing the powerful column of his throat, enhanced by the gold chain he wore. His clothes were ordinary and serviceable, so why did they

look so special on him? Cecilia was irrationally irritated. She dragged her eyes away and forced herself to concentrate on what he was saying. "I have had more success than I dared hope for in these times of financial stress throughout the world. I shall start with the best news of all. Not only have I raised all the monies we shall need for building the new 'factory' for the mass breeding of parasitoids, but we have also been promised the plane we shall need for their distribution over affected countries, and enough funds to adapt that plane to suit our uses."

Dolapo let out great shouts of delight. "So we'll be able to stick to our timetable. I shall be releasing millions of predators by March. Too late for this dry season, but there should be a bumper cassava crop in Africa next season."

"Not so fast, Dolapo." Ezeilo admonished his exuberant colleague with a smile. "That will depend on the success we have in the parasitoid rearing cages in the new 'factory'." He looked straight at Cecilia, and there was no smile on his face now, "That will depend on our new member of staff." His voice was as cold as ice, "By the way, I don't think I need to introduce Doctor Onochie to you, I think you all made her acquaintance at the party last night. I know I did," he added meaningfully.

Cecilia felt the blood suffuse her face. How dare he! How dare he sit there and audaciously remind her of last night! Holding her temper in check, she replied equally coldly, "That will depend on several diverse factors."

"Being?" Ezeilo asked sharply.

"Being, Doctor Obi, among others, whether we can persuade the quarantine officials to let the batch of second generation predator parasitoids into the country from the UK. That seems to be the first, all important factor, which," she looked round the other members of the team, "which seems to be causing us problems."

"Was, Doctor Onochie, was." To her ears Ezeilo's voice sounded very smug as he continued, "I am glad to be able to report that I solved that problem in Lagos yesterday. Continue Doctor Onochie."

Cecilia inclined her head and continued, "I see from the files that experiments have been carried out to avoid the mass rearing and releasing of unadapted predators, but I wish to carry those experiments a stage further before I start the mass rearing, to avoid any chance of failure. But I will discuss that with you at greater length if I may, Doctor Obi." She couldn't help a note of sarcasm in her voice as she added, "that is if you can spare the time." And she looked Ezeilo straight in the face as she said it. She thought a hint of a smile twitched at the corners of his mouth, as he replied equably, "I am at your disposal Doctor. But I must warn you that the experiments have been pretty extensive, as you would be aware if you had read his notes. Your predecessor was a brilliant scientist."

"And I'm not, I suppose," Cecilia thought to herself, her temper once more coming up to boiling point, but she replied coolly enough, "I am quite aware as I have read his notes, Doctor. However I consider that one of the factors was overlooked."

"Bear in mind, Cecilia that we don't want to hold up breeding any longer than neccessary," Dolapo smiled at her across the table.

"I know that, Dolapo and I am as anxious as anyone here to get this releasing programme underway as soon as possible, but that will only be when I am convinced that the parasitoids I am mass breeding will survive to do the job we intend that they shall do." Cecilia's voice was pleasantly modulated but very firm. Here she was on her own ground, gone was her initial nervousness. Ezeilo's loaded remarks had only served to make her more confident of her facts and conclusions.

"Point taken, Doctor Onochie, please continue."

"My last factor may contain many hidden factors. I refer to the 'factory' itself. From the brief study I have been able to make in the time at my disposal, I have one or two questions to ask about certain aspects of the actual structure, and one or two alterations to suggest that I am sure will add to the chances of success of the project." Cecilia was now totally with the obvious homework she had done in one day, impressed the others. The meeting became alive from that moment. Saying that he would interrupt his report in order to look at her criticisms and requests, as the matter was of urgent priority, Ezeilo called Ola to bring in the blueprints of the 'factory' for them all to study.

Cecilia had just risen to her feet to point out something on the plans when the door opened and Tim burst in. "Terribly sorry everyone, but my wretched alarm failed to go off." He looked at Ezeilo as he quickly slid into his empty chair, to meet two ice cold brown eyes that pierced his like gimmlets. "I've warned you before, Baker. I will not tolerate sloppiness, in clothing or manners, and being late for meetings is sloppiness in manners. As you have blamed your alarm clock on several occasions, I can only suggest that you get a new one," he looked directly at Cecilia as he said it. Her face burned. His insinuations must be plain to everyone. "Continue, Doctor Onochie, but I must warn you, you will not change my mind, nor the architect's I feel sure, about the safety of magnetic locks. They are the most efficient on the market." Cecilia could hardly contain herself, but only by the heaving of her bosom and the flash in her eyes did she show any signs of the mounting fury within her. "I know that, but I have experienced failure, and it can be catastrophic. How do you force a jammed magnetic lock, gentlemen?" Cecilia looked round the smiling faces at the table as she sat down, still controlling her anger with an effort.

Towards the close of the morning, Ezeilo brought the meeting back to his travels. And as they all rose to go to lunch, Cecilia realised that whatever else he was not, he could certainly make countries and foundations part with their money in a good cause.

Doctor Shivra came up to her as they were all having a final chat and picking up their bits and pieces, "Doctor Onochie, my wife gave me strict instructions to invite you to our Divali party next week." He fished in his pockets. "She gave me a card for you. Now, where can it have got to?" He smiled as he hunted through his pockets, and finally found it in his note book. "She says I am the most absent-minded professor she knows. She even phones me at the office to remind me that it is lunch-time and I must come home." He smiled again.

"Please thank your wife very much, I should love to come," Cecilia responded warmly.

"She will be delighted, as I am delighted to have you with us in the team. You are going to be a great asset I can see. Beauty as well as brains. Tim is a very lucky fellow." Cecilia couldn't help laughing, "You flatter me," she said.

Whether the sound of her laughter attracted Ezeilo's attention she never knew, but suddenly his voice rang out and its politeness hid the command in it. "I should like Doctor Baker and Doctor Onochie to stay behind, if they can spare a few minutes."

Tim glanced at Cecilia and pulled a face. We are in for trouble, it said. Cecilia, apart from a brief smile, had not had a chance to talk to Tim and she hadn't been sure that she wanted to. How could he have been late for this her first meeting with their boss? But now, after Ezeilo's insinuations she was wholly on Tim's side. She gave him a tender look as they went back to sit at the table.

Ezeilo, who had not moved from his seat, waited until Ola had closed the door on the others, then he pushed his chair back from the table, crossed his legs, and passed the pen back and forth, back and forth, through his long sensitive fingers, before he spoke.

"If I had known of the relationship between you I would never have consented to have Doctor Onochie on the program. I consider it a breach of etiquette that I was not informed by you, Baker."

"I didn't know Cecilia had got a job here until she told me. Then it was too late — you had already travelled." Tim looked aggrievedly at Cecilia, "She knows that it isn't what I wanted and . . ."

"I am not concerned with your wishes Baker. I am concerned with the success of this program, and I do not like having an engaged or married woman working on any project of mine." He looked at Cecilia, "Doctor Onochie is already familiar with my 'prejudices', I think she called them. Well prejudices or not, I do not approve of it for the reasons I have already given." He leaned forward over the table towards them. "How much more then do I disapprove of having two of my team engaged to each other. I am warning you both. At the first sign of either of you becoming inefficient or untrustworthy, I shall not hesitate to sack you." He stood up in a quick lithe movement. "I think that will be all for the moment. Good morning to you both." He turned away to his desk.

Cecilia was amazed at the difference between Ezeilo now and Ezeilo on the plane. He was a totally different person. True she had had a hint of it, but she would never have imagined in her wildest dreams that he could turn into this granite-like ogre in front of her. But she was not going to take that sitting down even if Tim was. "How dare you be so insulting to us. You don't own us just because we are in your group. And how dare you suggest that not only will I be inefficient because I am a woman but. . ."

"An engaged woman," Ezeilo turned from his desk to correct her.

"Well let me tell you, Mister Chauvinist par excellence, you will find no fault with my work I'll tell you that. And far from being a hinderance to Tim, I shall be an asset for we always used to discuss our work together and two. . ." Ezeilo interrupted, "heads are better than one, if you two must talk in unscientific cliches.

"Doctor Obi, "Cecilia was on her feet now, back straight and head held high, her body quivering with pent up fury, "ever since I have met you, you have gone out of your way to insult me and now you are insulting my fiance as well. I have had enough, I . . ." This time it was Tim who interrupted hurriedly with an angry look at Cecilia.

"Just a minute, Cecilia! Ezeilo, I'm sorry that I couldn't inform you about our relationship, but I am sure that you will find us both equal to our jobs. As Cecilia says, we have made a habit of working together in the past. I am sure we can do it to advantage here." He shot a warning look at Cecilia who looked as if she were about to explode at his conciliatory words to Ezeilo.

Cecilia couldn't read Ezeilo's expression as he said, "The situation is far from ideal, but because of the urgency of the program we will give it a try." His eyes were cold and blank. Then glancing at Cecilia, standing like an avenging angel, his gaze softened and a lopsided smile lifted up one corner of his mouth, making him look positively devilish to her furious eyes.

Cecilia picked up her briefcase and without a backward glance at either of the two men, made her way towards the door. Tim followed. They were just about to go through the door when Ezeilo's voice stopped them, "There is one thing more. No making out on duty please. We are all here to work."

Cecilia swept through the outer office, ignoring the astonished Ola and went straight to her office, tears of frustration and fury stinging her eyes. She didn't know which man she was angrier with. Ezeilo she knew was despicable, but how could Tim apologise and try to shut her up? It was past belief! She flopped down in her chair, put her head in her hands and wished with all her heart that she had never heard of RCA.

Tim's voice brought her head up with a jerk. "I'm sorry darling, but I just couldn't let you go on ruining both our chances." He looked so like a naughty boy, a lock of his straight blonde hair falling over his forehead, eyes uncertain, as he chewed his bottom lip in anticipation of her anger, that Cecilia melted. "Poor Tim," she said softly. "I'm afraid I've been a great disappointment to you but. . ."

"It's all right. Just of a bit of a shock that's all." He gave her an apology of a smile. "You've always seemed so calm, and now you are such a fire-brand I don't know how to cope with you." Cecilia sighed. "To tell the truth, I'm surprising myself as much as you." She rose to her feet tiredly. "I really am my parents' daughter after all, aren't? And I thought I had everything so under control!" A bitter note had crept into her voice.

Tim knew how much she had hated the emotional outbursts that had marred her childhood.

"No, you're not," he replied stoutly, "I expect it's just the strain of a new job." He took her in his arms, saying "And they do say that it's much easier to lose your temper in the tropics."

"But I was born here, and anyway I've only been back a few hours. Perhaps I never should have come."

"Of course you should have come." Tim put a hand under her chin. "You should have waited a little longer, that's all."

"All right, Tim, I've got the message," said Cecilia pulling her head away. "I suppose I should have just gone home to my family in Enugu and meekly waited until you called for me."

"That wouldn't have been such a bad idea."

"But there is nothing either of us can do about it now, so let's go and get some lunch, shall we?"

Suddenly I find I'm yearning for some pounded yam.'
She pulled out of his arms and picked up her bag.

"Me too." He put his arm round her shoulders,
and you must tell me all about your conversation
with Obi. I had no idea that you had spent anytime
with him last night."

"It wasn't last night, Tim. I was going to tell you.
We sat next to each other on the plane, neither of
us knew who the other was, and I'm afraid we didn't
exactly hit it off. He was the plane pest I was
telling you about." Tim's face looked incredulous,
then gloomy.

"Cheer up darling. Things can't get any worse,"
and Cecilia put her arms round his neck and kissed
him.

At that moment there was a knock on the door
and a face peered into the room, "Doctor Ono . . ."
It was Ezeilo's voice. Cecilia and Tim sprang apart,
Cecilia's startled eyes meeting a glance as frozen as
the Arctic. "I was about to suggest that we had a
working lunch." If possible, Ezeilo's voice was
colder than his eyes, "but I can see that you would
prefer to play." Ezeilo's head disappeared from view
and the door was slammed to. Tim looked glummer
than ever, "I thought you said that things couldn't
get worse," his voice was accusing. After all it was
she who had kissed him!

"Perhaps I was wrong, but I tell you one thing,
Tim, I am going to stand up to that impossible man
and neither you nor wild horses will stop me."

There was the light of battle in Cecilia's eyes as she marched out of the room. Sorry she'd come here? No, she certainly wasn't! The job was fascinating and she was more than capable of doing it. So she wasn't going to let a little thing like a totally unreasonable male chauvinist boss stop her.

Cecilia worked solidly through the afternoon and it wasn't until she had locked her office that she remembered that she had intended to phone Nike. Tim's remarks of the night before had gone deep, for she hated to hurt people's feelings, and if she had done so, however unintentionally, she would do her best to make ammends. Instead of phoning, Cecilia decided to drop in. A walk would do her good, blow the cobwebs away.

Nike met her with open arms, "Great. You've arrived at the best time. You can give me a hand with my two terrors. They are hurling the soap about the bathroom, and the water too I expect. Nothing on to spoil?" Cecilia shook her head, smiling. "Then come on we'd better get up there before they turn the bathroom into a lake. The nurse girl is there, but she lets them do exactly as they like. Besides I wouldn't miss their bath-time for the world, it's fun." Nike led the way to the upstairs bathroom. Chaos reigned, but it was happy chaos. Nike's children were full of fun and accepted Cecilia without a hint of shyness. The little girl, Bisi, was three while her brother, Seyi, was five. He looked exactly like his father, while Bisi favoured her mother.

By the time the children were dried, powdered and in their pyjamas, Nike and Cecilia were soaked, but Cecilia hadn't enjoyed herself so much for ages, and had splashed the water about with the best of them, much to the children's delight. It was a kind of water polo that Seyi had invented, Nike explained as she led Cecilia into her bedroom, insisting that she borrow a dry top at least.

"You're not a bit what I expected, you know," Nike volunteered, as they tidied their hair.

"As a scientist, or as Tim's fiancee?" Cecilia asked with a smile. Nike was so open and forthright but so nice with it, that she wasn't the least bit offended by the remark.

"Both I suppose." Nike looked at her, "But more as Tim's fiancée I think. I thought he would have chosen somebody much quieter, more docile than you." She sat down on the dressing-table stool.

"But I am quiet and fairly docile, normally."

"You quiet!" exclaimed Nike. "How can you be quiet with that gorgeous face and that gorgeous figure? Didn't you notice that you were the 'belle of the ball' last night? You had all the men eating out of your hand," she grinned at Cecilia as she added, "and all the women jealous."

Cecilia was shattered. Was Tim right after all? All the women jealous! She sank on to the bed looking distressed.

"It's all right, dear, don't look so worried. You'll do us all a power of good. Beauty as well as brains."

"Oh please, Nike, don't you start on that. I'm in enough trouble with my boss simply because I am a woman and have committed the heinous crime apparently, of being an engaged woman, and what is even worse in his eyes, engaged to Tim. Honestly, I sometimes can't believe that man is a Nigerian! But that isn't what I wanted to talk to you about." Cecilia leant forward, a worried frown marring her perfect brow, "Tim ticked me off last night good and proper. In fact we almost had a row." She looked down at her hands, "That's not quite true, we did have a row." Cecilia found it very hard to admit it. Her childhood experiences had bitten so deep into her psyche. Nike immediately became serious, "what on earth about?"

"About my bad behaviour," replied Cecilia, with a wry little smile that didn't quite reach her lovely eyes.

"But you were charming, haven't I just said it?" Nike sounded genuinely amazed.

"Not according to Tim, I wasn't. Oh, to my male colleagues maybe, but according to Tim, I insulted all of you wives by talking shop with the men. He said I should have joined the women: that the social side was important here and that I didn't act properly as his fiancée." Nike burst into peals of laughter, "He couldn't be more wrong. We were delighted to see one of our sex holding her own with our husbands. It's about time this institution had a top female scientist among them. And that you are an attractive woman too is an added bonus. To be truthful we were rather dreading you, thought you'd be a proper boring scientist."

"You really are serious, Nike? The women didn't find my behaviour insulting?" The frown that had creased her smooth forehead disappeared and this time her smile reached her eyes.

"Of course I'm serious." Nike got up. "Come on, you deserve a drink. Let's go and get one and then I'll make you sing for it by reading a bed-time story to the children."

Cecilia jumped up happily. "That sounds a wonderful idea. I could use a cool drink after that bathroom frolic, and I adore reading bed-time stories to children."

As they left the room, Nike said, "Come to think of it, if you aren't doing anything, why don't you stay to supper?"

"I'd love to, but you won't mind if I leave fairly soon after? I. . ."

Nike interrupted to finish the sentence for her, "have some work to do. I know." She grinned, as she held open the sitting-room door for Cecilia. "As I suspect that your ego is feeling a little deflated, shall I tell you what Dolapo said about you at lunch?" Nike went on, not waiting for a reply as she got two tall glasses out of the cocktail cabinet. "He was really impressed with the way you conducted yourself with Ezeilo at the meeting. He said that I only see the soft side of the boss, that he can be very intimidating and tough. Dolapo said you were terrific and he loved the way you looked, "Nothing of the intellectual 'bore' about her," he said. She rang the bell for the steward. "What would you like, Cecilia?"

"A coke, if you have it, please." Cecilia perched on the arm of one of Nike's comfortable chairs.

"Sure, easy," Nike turned to the steward who had just entered. "Two cokes, with plenty ice, please, Eke."

After the steward had left, Nike sank into another deep armchair. "Whewh! I'm bushed. Bringing up kids is hard work too, you know." She sounded a little on the defensive and Cecilia was quick to notice it, and at once put her new friend at ease. "You're telling me! I take my hat off to you mothers. Not only do you work much harder that most people, certainly longer hours, but it's such a selfless task. I really envy you, Nike. Your children are delightful and a real credit to you. It's easy to see that they have been brought up with a great deal of fun and laughter as well as discipline. I think you are very sensible not to work for the time being, as you don't need the money. I'm sure it's better for the kids, although it isn't traditional. I hope you don't come in for censure from the family?"

Nike was beaming with pleasure as Cecilia was

103

speaking. "Thank you. I try. And no, I don't have much trouble from the family. Dolapo has made it clear to everyone that he supports me in this." She looked seriously at Cecilia, "What about you and Tim? Do you plan to start a family as soon as you get married?"

Eke came back with two cokes from the fridge their bottles already covered with condensation, and a large bowl of ice. Nike rose to put a mass of ice in each tall glass and top it up with coke. "That should cool you down," she said, as she handed one to Cecilia.

"Thanks. That looks gorgeous," and Cecilia tasted its cold tangy freshness before she spoke again. "I want children of course, who doesn't, but. . ." she glanced across at Nike, who was sitting in what Cecilia came to know as her favourite position; sideways in the large chair with her pretty, plump legs over one of the arms and her back resting against the other. "I don't know why I'm talking to you like this," she said shyly. "I'm usually very reserved, but somehow I feel as if I've known you for years."

"That's exactly how I feel about you, so don't hesitate to bare your bosom to me. I'm as silent as the grave as well."

Cecilia couldn't help grinning for a moment, before becoming serious again. "Thanks. I know you'll respect my confidences, Nike. It's just that it's odd for me to feel free with you. I expect it's because I never had a close relationship with my mother."

"Why? Do you know?" Nike too was serious now.

"Oh yes. She never had any time for us. She was too busy quarrelling with father. They fought like cat and dog and destroyed each other, and their marriage, and in the end they parted." Cecilia didn't know how infinitely sad she looked at the memory of her childhood years, but Nike's heart went out to her.

"Poor you! How awful for you. You must have had a terrible childhood." There was a world of sympathy in Nike's voice. "I did. Oh there were happy moments of course, especially with granny, but. . ." Cecilia's voice trailed off for a moment as she was lost in those memories, then she looked up at Nike. "So you see, when I have children I want them to have a happier childhood than I had, and that means I shall have to devote a great deal of time to them. "But", she put her glass down, "I am a dedicated scientist and I don't think I could ever give it up entirely for home and children. I don't think I could ever do that, it isn't for me." She looked at Nike embarrassedly. "Now you'll think I've insulted you. I don't mean it like that, it's just that. . ."

"I'm not in the least bit insulted. Look, for me the housewife bit is totally satisfying, and luckily for me, Dolapo definitely doesn't want me to work while the children are young. I love cooking and cleaning and entertaining. But we aren't all like that and if I had a first class brain, and the education to make something of it, I'd want to fulfil my potential as well as have a family. I understand, I really do."

Cecilia smiled with relief, "I'm so glad you understand. Don't think I don't want children — I really do, but I'd like to wait for two more years: then I should be sufficiently established to take time off for children. I should hate to have them and leave them to a nanny all day."

"I know exactly how you feel. What's the problem then?" Cecilia hesitated before speaking. "Tim seems to have changed in the year we've been apart. From his remarks I know he is not considering my career, but only his. I think he feels, although he hasn't put it in so many words, that I should give up work as soon as we marry, and then I can be of use to him, mixing socially. He was very upset when I turned down Mrs Wagner's invitation to tea, because I would be working. He even thought I should have taken time off to go." It was out!

There was a pause. "And you've only found this out since you came here?" Nike asked after a while. Cecilia nodded.

"Why it's even old fashioned in the UK. Everyone expects their wife to work before she has kids. But you know dear, right from the start Tim has been socialising with the right people." Nike leant forward putting her hand on Cecilia's knee." I don't mean that nastily, it does help if the right people notice you. I like Tim, don't think I don't, but he's very ambitious and . . ." she stopped, and taking a quick drink of coke leapt to her feet. "Goodness! If those children are to have a story we'd better hurry up. Are you sure you want to come? You don't have to you know."

"Just you try to stop me!" Cecilia was already walking to the door. She turned to Nike. "Thanks, I . . ."

"No need to thank me," Nike cut in, with a grin. "Feel free to come and chew things over anytime."

"I might hold you to that."

"I mean it, Cecilia."

"I know you do. Come on, race you to the bedroom." And the two of them raced up the stairs like a couple of children themselves.

Chapter Five

Much to Cecilia's relief, the next week passed pleasantly. Her relationship with Tim appeared to be back to what it had been previously. Cecilia had been determined to make it so, by deliberately ignoring the uneasiness that the recent insights into his character had caused her. Their relationship once more was calm, warm and friendly, and wasn't that what she had always wanted as a basis for marriage?

At work she hardly saw Ezeilo, but on the few occasions they met in the labs he had kept conversation strictly to business, coldly impersonal. Knowing his attitudes to work and play, and how determinedly he kept them divorced from each other, she suspected that he might have felt considerably embarrassed, to find that the girl he had flirted with so outrageously on the plane, was a member of his staff. Not good for discipline! Well she was just as dedicated to her work as he was, so by not so much as a lift of an eyebrow did she step out of line. But her unruly heart still beat faster when she met him, although she would have died if he suspected it. It was something she was heartily ashamed of. She put all her efforts into her work and Ezeilo could not fault her. She was determined of that.

She was now in her own apartment and she had spent most of her free time moving in and making it as like home as she could manage. She was not as lucky as Tim with the furniture. It was not so elegant but she liked it as much, for in its own way it appealed to her: it was comfortable and homely. The three piece suite was well padded, but not overly so, and covered in a glazed chintz patterned with multicoloured flowers. She had a plain off-white carpet and cool lime-green curtains, well lined to keep out the heat of the day. Her bedroom had the lake view but she didn't mind, as she loved to gaze at it and watch the early morning birds as she did her aerobic work-out before breakfast. As the apartment was in the same block as Tim's, they often ate together, but she had insisted on a measure of independence and freedom and she was thankful that Tim had complied without protest. But mostly, she cooked for them both, and they enjoyed the easy companionship that existed between them.

She gave a little house-warming dinner party on her second evening in residence, just Tim, Nike and

Dolapo. She decided to prove that she had not forgotten her home cooking while she was abroad, and made a hot spicy palm oil stew. But to cool it down for Tim, she also made a banana and sweet potato casserole which consisted of alternate layers of par-boiled sweet potato slices and banana, seasoned with butter and white pepper, and cooked in orange juice. The sweet was a simple fruit salad topped with ice cream.

"That was a super meal, Cecilia," Nike said, as wiping her mouth on her napkin she sat back. "But wherever did you get that exotic sweet potato recipe from?"

"Ah, I have a super West Indian cook book that I picked up some time ago. It has mouth-watering recipes in it. I'll lend it to you if you like. "She turned to Dolapo and said, "Did you know Dolapo, that you can make pie-crust from cassava?" Dolapo shook his head, "I've got news for you, neither do our fellow countrymen."

"But the West Indians do." Cecilia rose to her feet, "Shall we leave the table and sit more comfortably?"

"I'll get the coffee, Cecilia," said Tim, walking towards the door. "Everyone take it black?"

"Milk for me, please, Tim", Nike answered, continuing, as she made herself comfortable in one of the armchairs, "You are as bad as the rest Cecilia. It's the same with all you scientists. All roads lead back to the project. We can't get away from cassava and maize when you Biological Control people are around." She grinned at them good-humouredly. "But don't mind me if you want to talk shop. I'm used to it," and Nike brought out some embroidery from her capacious bag.

"Thanks for your permission," Cecilia laughed, "but right now I want to talk about Mrs Shivra's Divali party. Is it very grand? What do I wear?"

"It is rather grand. She invites practically everyone on the campus. You'll love it, and it will give you a chance to meet everyone."

"I seemed to meet quite a few at your party," Cecilia remarked, sitting down next to her friend.

"That was nothing in comparison with the Shivra's do I can assure you. As to dress, put on something long and smashing." She took the coffee that Tim held out to her. "Thanks, the milk is just right. But she is a really nice person, so friendly and interesting and always willing to teach you how to cook Indian food. Mind you, for the Divali party all the other Indian ladies will cook at least one dish for her. It's a real spread."

"I must say I'm looking forward to it." Cecilia smiled up at Tim as she took her coffee.

"She works hard for her husband too, entertaining at least three times a week," Tim said, as he sat down beside Cecilia on the sofa.

"Yes," Nike agreed, "I couldn't do it myself. Dolapo doesn't mind. He says it's your work that counts with the provost, don't you darling?"

Dolapo nodded. "Of course that doesn't mean that we don't entertain, and you saw the Wagners at our party. I like the guy and his family, although Merribel must be an embarrassment to her father at times."

"I don't see why. She's a very pretty, attractive young woman," Tim defended, "and it must be hard for her out here with none of her own friends about. As a matter of fact she told me so the other night at your party."

"I noticed that she was rather subdued," Nike said, "but I put it down to another cause. You must know that she's fallen heavily for you Tim, and Cecilia's arrival must have been a real blow."

"Nonsense! You're being ridiculous, Nike," retorted Tim. Cecilia noticed he had flushed up to the roots of his hair. "It is just as I told you, darling," he glanced at Cecilia. "I was sorry for her and so I took the trouble to chat her up a bit. It did no harm. She's a sweet kid and I really like her."

"She certainly looks very charming," Cecilia put in. She could see that Tim was rattled and it was rather tactless of Nike to have spoken as she did. She was surprised; from what she already knew of Nike it was not like her.

"She is. She's going to Lagos at the week-end; her parents are sending her to stay at the American Embassy, to be with some people of her own age.

The ambassador's a great friend of theirs." He turned to Cecilia. "I've offered to give her a lift as a matter of fact, when I go down to pick up your parasitoids. Didn't I tell you?" Cecilia shook her head. At the mention of parasitoids the conversation turned to their program and Nike sat placidly doing her embroidery. She was obviously used to it.

After her guests had left, Cecilia tidied up, plumping cushions, removing cups and glasses and emptying ashtrays. As she did so, her thoughts turned to Merribel. She had said nothing in front of Nike and Dolapo, but secretly she thought that what Nike had said was true. Merribel seemed to have fallen heavily for Tim. What worried Cecilia was how much Tim had made made use of her to ingratiate himself with her father. She hoped with all her heart that none of the blame for Merribel's infatuation could be laid at his door! But poor Merribel. She seemed such a nice child.

The night of the Divali party arrived. Cecilia was very pleased that it was being held before Tim brought the precious parasitoids from Lagos, for once they were in her care, she knew partying would not be for her. She would be checking progress hourly. But she felt free to enjoy herself tonight.

She dressed with care, revelling in the pleasure of being able to wear such light clothing again. After a refreshing shower — she was constantly

113

having those — she put on a pair of simple cotton briefs and a cotton bra, prettily edged with lace. Then she slipped her head into a deceptively simply cut silk jersey dress in a deep shade of crimson. It had a low-cut back and clung to her narrow waist and slim hips, to fall in full folds to the hem just above her ankles. She put on a pair of high-heeled strappy gold sandals, a pair of gold bangles, gilt hoop earring and pulled her gold cross out from beneath the high front of the dress. Then she arranged her shining curls to her satisfaction.

She hardly needed mascara having long curling lashes of her own, but decided to use a little, and a black liner to add dramatic emphasis to her eyes, making them look even larger than they were. A dust of gold eye-shadow on her lids, a touch of dark red lipstick that matched her dress, and she was ready.

The Shivras lived in one of the big houses that Tim had pointed out to her on her first day. It was ablaze with lights: little bowls of oil with rags for wicks, lined the sides of the drive. They flickered and flared all round the house, for Divali, as well as being the Hindu New Year, is the Festival of Light.

Their hostess, who together with Doctor Shivra was waiting to welcome them at the door, was wearing a dark blue chiffon sari richly embroidered in diamante, palms together in the Indian greeting, saying, "Nemaste. I'm so glad that you could come Doctor Onochie. Happy Divali to you both".

As they made their way past their hosts across the terrazzo floor, from which all carpets and rugs had been removed, Cecilia hardly dare walk on the floor, for it had been most beautifully painted in a colourful and intricate pattern.

Their hosts had been standing at the entrance to one of the covered and netted verandas that flanked the house and ran the full length of the sitting-room. On looking round, Cecilia could see why Tim thought they were nice houses. They were beautifully designed for the climate: the floor to ceiling plateglass windows that also ran the full length of the sitting-room, were wide open. Mrs Shivra had placed the bar at one corner of the opposite covered verandah, in order to make as much room as possible for her guests. It was too crowded for Cecilia to see the room properly, something she was to do at a later date, but she got a general impression of it. There was a large painting of the god Shivra on one wall, some beautiful pieces of old Indian silver, and the best of the Western World in beautiful objects d'art. Kingfisher blue was the predominant colour, set off by some lovely pieces of glass. There were three tigers: one hung on the wall, snarling fiercely, and two more were stuffed and standing guard over the doors. Background music pervaded the atmosphere like incense, subtle, subdued, and very Indian.

There were already many people there. It was a gay scene, with all the usually more soberly dressed

Westerners in vivid colours. The Korean, Burmese and Malaysians were wearing their own national costumes, just as beautiful and rich as the Indian sari. Cecilia wished that she had worn her own lovely national dress. She soon left Tim's side to join the ladies. She was determined that Tim should be proud of her. She would be a good girl tonight, and not mention parasitoids or the lab.

When it was time to eat, the ladies were called first. "Western influence I feel sure, but I'm all for it," Nike whispered to Cecilia, who being very hungry by this time was only too willing to join the queue that was forming into the dining-room.

What an epicure's delight met her hungry gaze when she eventually was close enough to see the many dishes spread out before her on the large round table. She was handed a plate and cutlery, the latter wrapped in a paper serviette by Mrs Shivra's Indian maid, whose sari was simple and draped over her head, as tradition demanded of a servant.

"I've never seen anything like it. It all looks so gorgeous I don't know where to start," Cecilia said to Nike who was right behind her.

"Just follow the other ladies round and help yourself as you go, dear."

Nike pointed out some of the different dishes. It was a colourful spread with three different kinds of curry; a green curry with lots of green peppers in it, a red curry with tomatoes and red peppers and a

116

white curry with yoghourt.

"The white one is my favourite," said Nike taking a liberal helping, "and I love her yoghourt salad to take the heat of the curry away. It is always so beautifully seasoned, as well as having the usual tomatoes and cucumber in it."

Guided by Nike's more knowledgeable hands, Cecilia's plate was soon piled high with some familiar and many unfamiliar dishes, despite her having taken a modest amount of each.

"I'll never get through all this," Cecilia said, as they helped themselves to a glass of wine before making their way carefully back into the living-room.

"You'll surprise yourself, and manage a piece of the gorgeous moorish sweetmeat that will be served with coffee. It's a speciality of Mrs Shivra's, decorated with pure silver as thin as tissue paper. Makes you jump if you have any metal fillings in your teeth though. Your mouth becomes a mini-electric battery." Nike was making for the corner of one of the verandahs where there were already a few women sitting down attacking the food piled high on their plates.

As soon as Nike was settled in a comfortable chair she too set to with relish. Although Cecilia considered her plate to be full, Nike had managed to get much more on hers. Cecilia smiled at her friend, so plump and contented, and hoped that she and Tim would be as happy as Nike and

Dolapo obviously were. Thinking of Tim, she looked round for him and found him in the queue that the men were now forming. He caught her glance and she was rewarded with a look of warm approval. She was being a good girl, sitting with the wives. There was no sign of Ezeilo. She hadn't consciously looked for him, but glancing round the room now, she had seen no sign of his tall arresting figure. She half wanted him to come and half didn't, for he always managed to disturb her. But she would not have been a woman if she had not wanted him to see her looking her most feminine, in view of his opinion of women scientists.

She was soon captivated by the talk around her, mostly about food, under the circumstances. Recipes from all over the world were exchanged, and tips too, to which she listened eagerly. A lady from the Phillipines told her that if she wanted to make very good Chinese rolls with very thin pastry, she should first grease a frying pan very lightly and then dip a sponge into the batter and spread it very thinly over the base of the pan, only waiting until it started to curl up at the edges before removing it. Fancy using a sponge! Cecilia was intrigued and determined to try it out at the first opportunity. She had just decided that the wives out here must have a very interesting time learning about each other's ways, when a tall slim figure appeared at her side, and taking her almost empty plate out of her hands and depositing it firmly on a nearby table, said, "So this is where you have been hiding yourself." Then Ezeilo, for it was he, took her by the arm and pulled her to her feet. "We're having a very heated argument over the merits of our various ways of combating disease pests in tubers. Charles Hawtree thinks biological control is not as quick or long lasting as making the tubers genetically resistant to disease and pests. We need your brain on our side, or we may lose the battle." By this time he had her halfway across the room.

Cecilia was a in turmoil; furiously angry at the typically high-handed way he had just dragged her off without so much as a 'by your leave', but ridiculously pleased that he thought highly enough of her to want her to join in the argument. And all the time there was her physical awareness of the latent sexuality that exuded from him. He was looking devastatingly attractive too. Cecilia could see the admiring expressions on the womens' faces as he went by. He was in a pair of narrow, well cut dark grey trousers, worn low on his slim hips, with a pale grey, exquisitely embroidered shirt. It was open almost to the waist, and Cecilia caught the glint of his gold chain against his chest.

Suddenly, Cecilia was halted by a hand on her other arm restraining her. "What's happening, Cecilia? Why have you left the women?" It was Tim's voice.

Ezeilo had stopped, and glancing down at Tim,

said in a voice that brooked no argument, "I'm taking her to where I need her." He looked at Cecilia. "Come on."

Tim let go his grip at once, "In that case you can go, Cecilia."

"Thanks," Ezeilo replied, laconicaly, as he pulled on Cecilia's hand once more.

Cecilia was flamingly angry. She stopped dead. "Stop it! Both of you!" She kept her voice low, but it was full of controlled fury. "You are as bad as each other. You both think that as the little woman, I should do as you tell me, without considering my wishes at all." She turned flashing eyes on Ezeilo. "How dare you drag me off in that high-handed fashion in front of everyone. For your information I happened to be enjoying myself." She swung round on Tim, "And how dare you try to stop me just because you think I should stay with the women. You are as much a chauvinist as he is. And I thought that was the last thing you were." Here temper suddenly subsided leaving her oddly depressed.

Before Tim could speak, Ezeilo put an arm round her rigid shoulders. "I do apologise Lia, I was so carried away with the argument, and I needed you." His eyes were unaccustomedly gentle and tender. They did strange things to Cecilia, coupled with the fact that Ezeilo had used her christian name for the first time, and in that particular abbreviated form that only her much

120

loved grandmother had used: her mother's mother who had been the only calm and loving influence in her unhappy childhood. She suddenly had an illogical but overwhelming desire to be in the haven of Ezeilo's strong arms, to run her fingers over his thick curly hair and to bring his head down to hers so that she could reach his mouth with her eager lips. It was only for an instant that their eyes met, but it seemed to be a fusion of their spirits.

It was Cecilia who broke the spell, her chin jutting out belligerently, "Where is this Charles Hawtree then? I'll soon wipe the floor with him."

"I thought you would," Ezeilo replied with a boyish grin. For the first time since she had arrived, he reminded her of the handsome playboy who had pursued her on the plane. She turned to Tim. "Why don't you join us?" she asked, but he shook his head. It was obvious from his surly expression that he had not forgiven her. Cecilia laid her hand on his arm in a conciliatory gesture. "I'm sorry darling," she said quietly, "I really am." Cecilia meant it sincerely. She wished that she hadn't turned on him in front of Ezeilo. She would make it up to him later.

She was unaware that a pair of baby-blue eyes had been watching the altercation closely, and as soon as she had moved away, a tiny figure in a powder-blue sari, which made her look like a wraith, came up to Tim's side, slipped her arm through his and led him into a far corner of the room. Tim's ruffled feathers were about to be smoothed.

After all, Cecilia was glad that Ezeilo had called her into the argument for it was a good one. It ended with coffee and sweetmeats and much laughter and once again she thought what a nice bunch the scientists were. She wished that Tim had joined them, although he didn't enjoy discussions as much as she did.

Not by one little glance did Ezeilo show that he thought she looked nice, and sitting back on the ornate bamboo sofa beside him, she felt oddly piqued. Well you wanted him to treat you as a serious scientist and now that he is, you're displeased. Just like a woman, she thought ruefully, as she bit into the delicious milky sweetmeat. If she had many of these, she'd be as fat as butter, but they were the perfect end to the curry meal.

"A propos of what we were just arguing about, I'm going to our experimental farms outside Abeokuta on Saturday. Have you been there yet?" Ezeilo asked her. Cecilia shook her head, "No, I've been too busy catching up on the job here, but I plan to go soon. Tim said he would take me."

"Why don't you come with me then?" He stirred his black coffee, "or would your fiancé object?" There was a sardonic twist to his strong mobile mouth.

"Of course he wouldn't," she replied quickly, thinking that as long as she was going with the boss

122

it would be all right by Tim. "He's going to Lagos at the week-end to be at the airport on Monday morning bright and early, to pick up the parasitoids." Her eyes, alight at the thought of her parasitoids, looked up into Ezeilo's and the conversation hung suspended as they were lost in each others gaze. Cecilia felt strangely breathless. Then his deep voice broke the spell. "You really are excited about those parasitoids, aren't you?" She nodded, unable to speak for the lump that had suddenly formed in her forehead and it was almost a lover's caress. "You look like a little girl about to be given a present." His mouth, now soft and warm and sensual, mesmerised Cecilia, as her own gentle lips quivered into an answering smile.

So he had noticed her! She felt absurdly pleased.

"Cecilia, if you've finished talking shop, I want to introduce you to a very good friend of mine." It was Nike's voice that brought Cecilia back to reality and looking up at her startled, Cecilia caught a knowing look on her friend's face. It vanished in a flash, so quickly in fact that she could not have sworn that it had really been there at all.

"That is if you can spare her, Ezeilo?" Nike asked lightly.

Ezeilo rose lazily to his feet, "Take her away then. It's time she was a good girl and mixed with the women again." He paused, the cold, cynical note hardening his voice once more. "To please her chauvinist fiance."

Cecilia felt the blood rushing to her face from a mixture of embarrassment and annoyance. Ezeilo was much too observant and why did he have to spoil things by being sarcastic, just when she thought they seemed to be friends?

He took her hand and placed a kiss in the upturned palm. Cecilia felt a delicious sensation fly through her body to come to rest at the core of her femininity. He folded her fingers over the place that he had kissed, as if to capture that kiss for her, as he said, "I'll pick you up at seven a.m. And for goodness sake wear sensible clothing for trekking over the farms."

Oh! She could make neither head nor tail of him. He had her running the full gamut of her emotions in the space of a few hectic seconds, drat him! "Don't worry, I won't forget my topee," she answered sarcastically — topees having gone out with the ark.

"Good." He grinned at her.

"What goes between you two?" Nike asked, as she took Cecilia to meet her friend. Nike would rush in where angels feared to tread!

"Nothing goes," Cecilia replied airily. "I can't stand the man."

"You could have fooled me," Nike muttered to herself.

The friend in question turned out to be an American girl of about Cecilia's own age who, Nike said, as she introduced her, was the women's hang-gliding champion of the United States.

She didn't look at all as **Cecilia** expected a hang-glider to look: she was a tiny fragile person with long black hair and a heart-shaped face.

"Oh I do envy you being able to hang-glide. It must be a lovely sensation with those large wings strapped on to you, soaring silently over the country, just like a bird. How did you come to take it up? I thought it was a man's sport," Cecilia said to the girl, who turned out to be Charles Hawtree s wife.

"It is mainly a man's sport, but there is a growing number of our sex taking it up. I had five brothers and I was the only girl. Need I say more?" Megan Hawtree grinned. Cecilia laughed. "Lucky you. I wish I had some brothers."

"I can imagine. But five is rather over-doing it don't you think?" Megan shook her head at the steward who was offering her another drink.

"You must miss it out here." Cecilia too refused another.

"No, I practise most weekends up in the hills near Iseyin."

"I can't imagine what the villagers think as they see you soaring about," laughed Nike. "They must have been scared out of their wits at first."

"They were, but I think they are used to me now. Charles hang-glides too. It makes a nice change to get away at the weekends."

"Did I hear my name being taken in vain?" questioned a male voice. "Time to go I think. Come

125

along, Megan darling." Charles turned to Cecilia, "Nice arguing with you. We must do it again some-time."

"Delighted. Anytime," Cecilia replied with a smile. She turned to Megan. "It's been most interesting meeting you, I hope we can get together sometime. Maybe at Nike's." She turned to smile at Nike, who was pleased that her two friends hit it off so well.

"We'll have a hen party one night when the boys are attending a meeting somewhere. Unless of course you've gone to it too, Cecilia," Nike said. "Oh dear, I keep forgetting that you're one of them."

"I take that as a compliment." Cecilia linked her arm through Nike's. "And now I think it's time for us to go home. Lets find our menfolk."

Chapter Six

The following Saturday Cecilia woke very early feeling ridiculously happy. She wanted to be ready for Ezeilo. He wasn't going to find her wanting. She ate a hearty breakfast, having no idea when she would eat next, for she was determined that however tough the going was, tramping over rough ground, she was not going to fall by the wayside. With a good helping of grapefruit, omelette, toast and coffee in her stomach, she felt fortified to meet any eventuality. She had put on jeans, patched and faded, but a favourite pair of hers, and a cotton T-shirt with short sleeves. She had chosen a white one to reflect the heat of the mid-day sun. The mist would take some time clearing, but then it would be hot. On her feet she put an old pair of flip-flops, but she was taking with her a pair of heavy gum boots that she had brought home from the office the night before. A wide-brimmed straw hat that she had bought cheaply from a Hausa trader, completed her outfit.

On glancing at her watch she saw that it was ten-to-seven. She must hurry. No time now to stop on the way down and wish Tim a safe journey to Lagos. She picked up a large light-weight shoulder bag to carry her notebook, camera and the minimum of equipment she might require for the collection of specimens, and rushed down the stairs and out into the drive way to await Ezeilo's arrival.

As she had known he would, he arrived on the dot of seven. It was light now, but he still had his headlights on to combat the heavy mist. He stopped the landrover and held open the door for her.

"Good morning, Lia." He looked at the heavy gumboots in her hand and smiled. "I see you took me at my word. But don't you think a stout pair of shoes would have been more comfortable? The ground will be fairly dry yet you know." His mouth quivered into a smile, which turned into a broad grin when Cecilia answered, "I am perfectly well aware of that thank you, but I am also aware that in all probability snakes of many kinds are sure to be lurking among the stalks of corn and cassava bushes, and I have a terrible fear of snakes."

Ezeilo shook his head. "I don't believe it. You are not invincible after all, you do have an Achille's heel."

"Doesn't everyone?" Cecilia answered with some asperity as she flung the boots and her bag in the back of the landrover.

"Do I detect signs of morning bad temper?" he said looking at her quizzically.

"As it happens, I woke up feeling very happy this morning," Cecilia said, without thinking, as she settled herself in the high but comfortable seat next to him.

"Did you now! I wonder why?" drawled Ezeilo. It was a question, but the tone of voice suggested that Ezeilo already knew the answer — and found it gratifying.

But Cecilia's mind was on the trip ahead and she was determined that he was not going to spoil it for her by baiting her, not in any other way. This was a scientific excursion in the execution of her work. Nevertheless she was acutely aware of him sitting beside her. He was in brief shorts, which exposed the powerful length of his legs. She could see the strong muscles of his thighs and calves. Like her, he wore a simple T-shirt, white, old and frayed. He had an old bush cap on his head, spurning the smart, moulded-mesh, peaked variety issued by the authorities. On glancing down at his feet on the pedals she could see that he had on a pair of thick socks and heavy shoes. Not elegant attire at all, and yet he gave the impression of a sophisticated man of the world who would be at home in smart society anywhere. What a mixture he is, Cecilia thought, and what an enigma. Would any woman ever be able to plumb the depth of his personality?

Ezeilo treated her like a colleague. She might

have been a man. They talked of work all the way to Abeokuta and Cecilia began to feel totally relaxed in his company and stimulated by his mind. She could see why he was Group Leader. Once on the subject near to his heart his concentration was total. But more than that, he had the quality that all leaders should have; the ability to inspire those working with him. If it were possible, Cecilia felt even more involved with the research than before.

The time flew by and before they knew it they were driving through the outskirts of Abeokuta.

"Do you know anything of the history of the Yorubas?" Ezeilo asked.

Cecilia shook her head, "Not much, only what little I learnt in school. I'm very ignorant, I'm afraid."

"Most of us are. We know more about the outside world than we do about our own peoples. Mind you I think our educational system is improving with each generation. I'm sure today's kids know more already about their country than we do." He raised an eyebrow saying "Would you like to go back to school for a minute or two?" She nodded, smiling. "The Yorubas were constantly fighting each other and at the time I am speaking of, the Egba tribe who were scattered around the district weren't doing so well, so they left their villages pursued by the Ibadans, among others, and in fleeing came upon this place. You can see already how hilly it is. They weren't stupid, and noticing the Ogun river and the hills, they decided that this might be a good spot to stay. They had water and they had the protection of the hills. They were even more pleased when they discovered that under the biggest rock on the highest hill," he pointed to his right, "you can see it now, over there. It's called the Olumo Rock, by the way. I'm sure you must have heard of that — there were caves big enough to shelter them all, and which were easy to defend. Would you like to go and see it? "

Cecilia nodded, "I'd love that, if we can spare the time."

"Sure, it won't take us long. It's better to do it now as it is quite a climb, exhausting in the heat of the day, even for a slim young woman like you." He turned off the main road and the landrover started to climb. "They made this into a shrine later on as it had saved the tribe. Now they have fenced it off because litterbugs were messing it up, but it's still worth a visit."

"Why is it called Olumo Rock? " she asked, peering out of the window now, camera in hand.

"It means 'God made' in Yoruba, and Abeokuta means 'under the rock'. It all makes sense, doesn't it?" He glanced at her camera poised. "Would you like me to stop a minute?" he asked.

"It's all right thanks, I think I can manage. I have a fairly fast film in it.' '

"Are you as professional a camera enthusiast as

you are a scientist?" Ezeilo queried, as he gathered speed, Cecilia having taken her photo.

"Ah!" She exclaimed, "I have at last managed to persuade you that an engaged woman can behave professionally at her work. I don't believe it!" But she felt a rush of pleasure through her veins.

"I wouldn't say that exactly. You may still fall by the wayside," he said as he threw her a cynical glance. "Shall we just say that up until now you have been fairly satisfactory." Cecilia ground her pearly white teeth. "If you weren't driving I'd throw something at you." But she couldn't help laughing, and they were both still laughing when they got out of the landrover to climb up to the rock.

On their return from the rock, hot and sticky despite the early hour, Ezeilo got a couple of soft drinks out of the cold box, which refreshed them before setting off again on their way to the farms.

As they drove through the town, Cecilia took more photographs of the old market, especially of the adire cloths, for which Abeokuta is so famous.

"Europeans tend to associate Africans with rather garish colours, but the Yorubas wore only this indigo dyed cloth for years and years." Ezeilo was a fund for the knowledge that Cecilia found fascinating. "It's very fashionable again nowadays – and very expensive Nike tells me." Cecilia spoke as she put her camera away in the bag behind her.

"Thank you for making this such an interesting day, Ezeilo," she added shyly.

He looked down at her, his strong features softened by the expression in his eyes. "My pleasure," he answered lightly.

As Ezeilo told Cecilia, they had not much farther to go, the farms being only a few kilometres outside the town. Sure enough, in under half an hour Ezeilo turned on to a bush laterite road, and having bumped along it for about half a kilometre, the tyres sending up a smoke screen of red dust behind them, he pulled up to the side of the road under a large shady mango tree.

"That will help to keep our transport cool," he remarked as he leapt out of the landrover as agile as a cat. "We'll come back here for our lunch. We should have seen what we want to by then." He fished an old rucksack and Cecilia's bag out of the boot. "Here you are, Lia. Is there anything in it that you want to leave behind?" Grinning wickedly he added, "articles of feminine toilet perhaps?"

"Do I look as if I've brought anything so stupid on a trip like this?" Cecilia laughed, "Can't you see that I am completely without make-up?"

"I can and even more beautiful too" His eyes held hers for a moment, in a deep sexual encounter that left Cecilia weak at the knees, but she pulled her eyes away firmly, and ignoring his helping hand, leapt to the ground unaided. There was going to be none of that nonsense on this trip! Not if she could help it!

"Once at work, Ezeilo was merciless; they trudged through fields of maize, often towering above Cecilia's head, examining leaves, taking samples and making notes. Cecilia was to take the notes whilst Ezeilo collected the samples. "Fair division of labour, don't you think?" Ezeilo had asked, before they started on the first farm.

"You should have seen this farm last year. Three quarters of the crop was destroyed by mealie bugs, and with the drought last year, I doubt if they would have had any crop at all this season without Dolapo bringing the predators here. Of course we won't have quite the same success with the cassava as we haven't yet got the specific predators for the green spider mite."

"Anytime now, Doctor Obi," Cecilia responded, for a moment thinking of Tim on his way down to collect the precious batch from London. She wondered idly if Merribel would go with him to collect them. She thought not somehow. She suspected that Merribel would hate creepy crawlies.

"Lia!" Ezeilo spoke sharply," Wake up! Take this down will you?"

Feeling very guilty for letting her mind wander, Cecilia did as she was told, and from then on she gave her whole concentration to the job.

By the time Ezeilo had decided that he had enough data and specimens, and that the experiment was going well Cecilia's clothes were sticking to her, soaked with sweat, her legs were aching and she had blisters on both heels from her gum boots. But not a murmur of complaint escaped her parched lips. Ezeilo had been far too engrossed to notice her. She was just a notebook and pencil to him, until they were nearing the landrover.

"Cecilia, you're limping."

Cecilia had done her best to hide it, but her blisters were now agony. "It's nothing, just a little blister or two I suspect. I shouldn't have worn these boots, but we did see a couple of snakes," she said, vindicating herself.

"We did, did we? I did not, it just so happens." His face relaxed from the severe lines and angles imposed on it by his total absorption in the work. "I've got a first-aid kit in the back. As soon as we reach the landrover I want to take a look at those blisters."

"It's nothing really."

"That is an order, Doctor Onochie. No subordination. I'm in charge of this outfit. And call me a male chauvinist if you dare!"

Cecilia smiled inspite of the pain, "Not this time. You are in charge, as my boss. I would never dispute that on the job, but my blisters are my own affair and. . ."

Ezeilo interrupted her, "There you go again. If I wasn't so hot and tired I'd put you over my knee and spank you." He looked at her, and the wicked sparkle in his eyes turned to consternation as he saw the pain mirrored in her own. He put a strong arm round her waist, saying gently, "But instead I shall carry you the rest of the way." Before she realised what he was doing, he had suited actions to words and she was in his arms and being held close to his chest. For one blissful moment she let her head rest in the curve of his neck before struggling to get free. Her struggles were in vain, for he was much stronger that she and equally determined to have his way.

True to his word, on getting to the landrover he deposited Cecilia on the seat and then eased off the offending gum boots. She was amazed at his gentleness. Then his fine hands with their long sensitive fingers carefully held each foot in turn as he examined the blisters, shaking his head in amazement when he saw how large and broken they were. "You should have told me, I could at least have lent you my socks."

"And run the risk of spoiling your research?" Cecilia shook her head, "If we had been on a pleasure trip I would have told you, but the job had to be done. Ezeilo looked at her, the light of admiration in his eyes taking the sting out of his words, "As tough as a man, eh, my little intellectual? Perhaps you really are an intellectual after all, and not the good-time girl I took you for." Cecilia didn't even mind that he had taken her for a good-time girl, a suggestion that at any other time she would have objected to most fiercely. But now it was enough to bask in the admiration in his eyes. She did not say a word.

Ezeilo cleaned the blisters, disinfected them, and with a warning that it was going to hurt, protected them with two layers of New Skin, a liquid that did just that — dried over the blisters, forming a protective transparent skin. The pain brought tears to Cecilia's eyes and she shut her lids tightly to prevent them from escaping, but all the same one or two salty rivulets made their way down her dusty cheeks.

After he had slipped her slip-slops over her feet, Ezeilo opened the cold box and took out two icy cold beers. "I don't expect you usually drink beer, but I can assure you there is nothing so refreshing as a cool lager when you are hot and dehydrated. We in this country happen to make lager very well. He handed her a glass without more ado. When they had quenched their thirst, he brought out legs of peppered chicken, french bread and butter and tomatoes.

Cecilia discovered that inspite of her large breakfast she was very hungry and ate heartily. She had expected something much more frugal and she suspected that when Ezeilo was out in the field on his own it would be more frugal, if he stopped to eat at all. As if reading her thoughts Ezeilo said, "You are probably thinking that I have put on this spread especially for you — that I don't bother with food when I'm on my own out here, but I'm a great

137

believer in eating a decent meal in the fields. It's tiring work under difficult conditions and I have known strong men faint under the strain of it."

"Really," Cecilia replied, unconvinced.

"Really" — my doubting Thomasina, he grinned infectiously, showing his fine white teeth, sensual grooves forming down the sides of his nose and mouth, "because I have been one of those strong men."

"You haven't! Not you?" Cecilia's mouth began to twitch as she tried to hide her own grin. "So you have an Achilles' heel too."

He nodded, "Letting your blood sugar get too low, that's what does it. But you, my tough little intellectual, not only got through it, but with blisters as well" He fed her with a particularly succulent piece of chicken, which she ate with relish, licking her lips with her tongue when she had finished it. "But sometimes," continued Ezeilo, wiping her mouth gently with a clean serviette, "my efficient, tough, intelligent, intellectual only looks about four years old, like she does at this moment, her dirty face streaked with salty tear stains, staring at me so seriously with her brown eyes, which are much too big to be true."

Cecilia thought he was going to kiss her, but instead he merely took her plate from her and started to pack up the picnic things. She told herself that she was glad. She wasn't a good-time girl, happy to accept cheap kisses that had no meaning. She determined to be very cool and aloof on the journey back. If Ezeilo noticed her withdrawal, he made no remark about it and they spent the journey home summing up their conclusions from the evidence that they had amassed.

When they turned into the gates of RCA, Cecilia felt a cloud descend on her spirits like a large grey blanket. The day was nearly over.

"I don't know about you, Lia, but I think I owe it to myself to relax a bit now. After all it is the weekend and we have done a good job. What do you say to our dumping our stuff and spending the rest of the afternoon at the pool?" he looked at his watch, "it's half-past four already."

Miraculously the cloud lifted and Cecilia was once more in good spirits. "I think that's a lovely idea. I'll have to deal with the specimens first, but that won't take me long."

Ezeilo drove straight to the labs and then arranging to meet at the pool, they went their separate ways.

When Cecilia looked in the mirror, having slipped home to pick up a bikini, she couldn't believe the sight that met her eyes. She certainly had a dirty face. It was covered in red dust, streaked by her tears and sweat. What must Ezeilo have thought of her? And yet he had been nice to her. Well, he had certainly seen her at her worst. She must shampoo her hair and have a shower before joining him at the pool.

When Cecilia arrived at the pool, her hair was once more shining clean, and a quick shower had cleansed and refreshed her body. The New Skin that covered her blisters would protect them from the water, so she had no worries on that score she thought , as she quickly stepped into her turquoise and white striped bikini in the changing room. Then picking up her towel and bag she went in search of Ezeilo, sure that he would be there before her.

At first she didn't see him, then she glimpsed his handsome head sticking out of the water, surrounded by all the children in the pool who were shrieking with delight. Once again he amazed her. Automatically she had been searching for him in the deep end or on the diving board, or at least swimming strongly wherever he was. It never crossed her mind that he would be entertaining the children.

"You'll catch a fly if you don't watch out," Nike said, at her elbow. "Penny for them?" Cecilia smiled, "They aren't worth it. But if you must know, I was thinking what a complex person Ezeilo is. I thought he was the sort of man who wouldn't have time for children." The two girls started to walk along the side of the pool.

"I think you've got that man all wrong. He loves kids and my kids adore him. He's their favourite 'uncle'." Nike made for a groups of chairs where Cecilia could see Dolapo sitting reading a newspaper.

"Come and join us," Nike said, sitting down on a lounger. "We won't be here much longer. The sun is almost setting and that means it's time to get the kids home for their supper."

"Thank you, I'd love to, but I arranged to meet Ezeilo here so. . ." At Nike's raised eyebrows, Cecilia added shortly, "We have been working together all day on the farms at Abeokuta. Feeling hot and sticky, he thought a swim would do us good. That's all, Nike." Dolapo looked up eagerly from his paper. "How did it go? I'm sorry that I didn't come with you, but I do so look forward to my Saturdays with the family when it's at all possible, and Ezeilo said he didn't need me."

"It went very well, and I was really impressed. I think we've undoubtedly got a winner." Cecilia had sat down on one of the slatted chairs by the round table which was covered with the Solaru's swimming things. She was just about to ask Dolapo about a point that she wanted to clear up, when she heard her name called. Ezeilo was standing up in the pool, leaning his strong arms on the side, and shaking water out of his hair, "If you sit there you will be talking shop with Dolapo, and I thought we'd decided it was playtime now." He held out his arms. "Come on in." With a smile, Cecilia got up from the table, and putting her things on the chair, ran lightly to the pool. But not into Ezeilo's waiting arms. She dived in quickly, then came up beside him, laughing. He caught her to him swiftly.

141

"I couldn't wait a minute longer to hold you in my arms. You look nice enough to eat in that whisp of a bikini," he whispered in her ear before he started to nibble it. But Cecilia pulled her head away quickly, "Oh no you don't, Doctor Obi!" she was half laughing.

"Oh yes I do, Doctor Onochie." Ezeilo held her even closer until she could feel the hardness of his lithe body pressing against hers. The more she struggled, the more aware she was of his virile masculine body. She could feel his growing excitement hardening him against her thighs. But he didn't get a chance to nibble her ear again — with one mighty effort she wriggled free and swam swiftly away. He pursued her like a flash, cleaving through the water with a powerful crawl and reaching the other end of the pool before she did. But Cecilia was a good swimmer too, and turning swiftly was away before he realised it. They swam fiercely for many lengths of the fast emptying pool, each, Cecilia suspected fighting his own demons. She at any rate was shocked at the feelings the closeness of Ezeilo's near-nude body had roused in her, and angry with him for taking such liberties with her, knowing full well that she was engaged to Tim. Had he no morals? Was he prepared to use anyone to satisfy his animal passions? But by the time she had swum a few lengths, the fierce exciting feeling surging through her body lessened. When they finally came to rest at the shallow end of the pool, she made a point of distracting his attention. "Oh Ezeilo, just look at the sun, have you ever seen anything like it?" It was indeed a marvellous sight: the sky had turned to dusty grey in the middle of which sat an enormous dull orange ball, dwarfing the landscape underneath.

They stood there silently looking at the beauty spread out before them like a magnificent painting, neither wanting to break the spell; each equally aware of the other's body and the electric currents flowing between them despite the fact that they were not in contact.

The spell was eventually broken by Nike's cheerful voice calling out goodbye, as she shepherded her two tired but happy offspring on their way.

Ezeilo swung his large frame out of the pool with a lithe grace and turning, held out his hand to help Cecilia, but she was again too quick for him, as with a grace that more than matched his own, she too jumped out of the pool. He looked her up and down, taking in every detail of her lovely body, barely concealed by her turquoise and white striped bikini. "You should wear that more often," he said huskily. "It suits you." Cecilia turned her back on him, walked swiftly to the table which Nike and Dolapo had just vacated, and picking up her matching turquoise towel, tied it round herself like a wrapper.

"How about a drink, my slender maid?" Ezeilo asked, when he had vigourously towelled himself dry.

"I'd love one, under certain conditions," Cecilia answered seriously.

Ezeilo swung a leg over the chair opposite her and leaning on its back to face her, said, "Fire away."

"Not only am I a serious scientist, I am also a serious person — and an engaged one. Not all women are empty-headed play things, Ezeilo."

"Aren't they?" there was a cynical twist to his mouth.

"No, they are not," Cecilia replied firmly, "I've really enjoyed my day with you, so please don't spoil it all by making cheap advances to me."

For a moment there was such an angry glitter in Ezeilo's eyes that she was afraid he might hit her. He was capable of it she felt sure, but then he relaxed and smiled disarmingly as he said blandly, "I will agree to your terms. No cheap passes, you said?" he continued before Cecilia could speak, "but in return I shall expect you to do me the honour of having dinner with me." Again Cecilia was about to speak, but he held up his hand. Please don't refuse because it would be the perfect end to a perfect day. "His eyes did not plead with her to accept. He was not the sort of man that would ever plead with a woman, but she thought her message had got across, and to tell the truth, she had enjoyed his company, and dinner together would round off the day.

144

"Well, all right, thank you. As long as you have promised to behave." He nodded, but there was a strange yearning in his eyes as he went to order their drinks.

The pool was deserted now, save for a few groups of people sitting at the surrounding tables. The water took on the soft grey of the sky, and the sun was mirrored in its still waters. Cecilia, sipping her ice-cold chapman, gave a little sigh of contentment. The view was beautiful, the winking lights of Ibadan in the distance and the sky now black with the bodies of hundreds of bats that had risen from the forest below, to fly slowly and deliberately away in search of food.

"I've watched those bats almost every evening since I've been here," Cecilia said. "They fascinate me. Why do they always fly in the same direction?"

"It is strange, isn't it? I don't know the answer. You'll have to ask an expert, but maybe it is as simple an answer as that the best food lies in that direction." She giggled, "You could be right at that."

Ezeilo proceeded to put himself out to amuse and entertain her in a charming way, and if something electric had gone out of the atmosphere between them, Cecilia told herself that she was glad.

They lingered lazily over their drinks until the wind blew a little cool. They then went their separate ways, to change for dinner.

Cecilia washed her hair again because of the chlorine in the pool, but took the precaution of applying a generous amount of conditioner. Ezeilo had said that he was taking her into Ibadan to a good Lebanese restaurant he knew. She decided on something short but dressy. The one suitable garment that she possessed was a little black crepe dress.

After yet another shower, she rubbed her favourite body lotion all over her body. It was the same scent as the perfume she would wear. She had no intention of wearing the perfume that Ezeilo had bought her. That would be asking for trouble. Neither would she wear her favourite exotic perfume *Opium* by Yves Saint Laurent. Instead she chose *L'air du Temps,* a delicate flower-based perfume with just a hint of sophistication. She hardly ever used nail varnish because of the nature of her work, so she merely buffed her filbert-shaped nails to a soft shine. She decided to wear her strappy black sandals rather than her gold. And finally, to prevent too sombre a look, she took a pale pink clutch bag and tucked a large pale pink rose in the belt of the dress, which had a low-cut neckline, three-quarter sleeves, and a bodice and skirt which were draped to show off the soft lines of her figure.

She decided to put on some make-up: just her usual black mascara, eye liner and a lipstick.

She had taken great pains with her appearance.

She was still smarting a little from being called intellectual.

On the stroke of half past eight, there was a ring at her door, as Cecilia had expected. She opened the door to an immaculate Ezeilo. She felt suddenly shy. He was so tall and had such an overwhelming aura of masculinity about him. He was freshly shaven, the scent of his after-shave heavy about him. He was not in the conventional shirt and tie that Cecilia had expected, but wore a pure silk cream shirt with large full sleeves gathered at the wrist. The neck was edged by a wide collar and cut in a vee to button low down his chest. It made the perfect setting for his gold St. Christopher pendant which gleammed brightly against his torso. With it he wore tight fitting black velvet pants which clung to his limbs like an extra skin. He looked devastatingly romantic, his handsome, proud head and magnetic eyes topping it all. Remembering his frayed old shorts and T-shirt of the morning, a twinkle came in to Cecilia's eyes. "Quite a change," she said, smiling up at him.

He let his glance run wild over her body for a moment before he too grinned. "You too," he replied.

Cecilia had not been off campus at night since her arrival, and she looked out of the window eagerly as they approached the city, passing many road-side markets on their way. Many of the stalls were lit up with brightly coloured neon strips and others, poorer ones, by a solitary storm lantern. Their goods were attractively displayed, sometimes be-lying the laws of gravity: Especially those piled on the trays balanced precariously on child's head.

"For these traders it's not only their livelihood it's their social life as well. I think they'd be very bored and lonely if they had to live our sort of lives." Ezeilo hooted at a pedestrian who had just dashed out in front of the car as he spoke. "Being able to read like us makes a terrific difference. You no longer need other people as much."

"Of course you're right, but even so, among our own social strata there are quite a few who could occupy themselves, but are not happy unless they are with other people." She paused before continuing. "I think Tim is a bit like that. Oh not if he has work to do," she said hastily, lest Ezeilo should get the wrong impression.

"He's not as dedicated as you are, Lia." Cecilia sensed his disapproval, "I don't agree," she rushed to defend Tim, "he's very ambitious and . . . "

"I'll give you that," drawled Ezeilo, interrupting her, but for position and power. Whereas you, my little intellectual do not care a hoot for either of those; you care passionately about bettering the world through scientific research." He did not take his eyes off the road as he spoke. "What I don't understand is how someone who is so passionate about her work can settle for such a cold fish for a fiancé."

"I don't think that is any of your business," Cecilia answered stiffly.

"But, of course, I remember you told me on the plane what you thought was the right basis for marriage." She saw his mouth turn up at the corners, "I'm afraid I don't agree."

"And you are such an expert on matrimony, I suppose." There was a wealth of sarcasm in Cecilia's voice.

"Perhaps not, but on how to avoid it, I certainly am." There was more than a hint of laughter in his voice that annoyed her. "That I can well believe," she replied icily.

"Would you care to see Ibadan stretched out like a glittering carpet at your feet?" Ezeilo abruptly changed the subject. Cecilia suspected that it was deliberate, as their discussion had become too personal, but she was more than happy to go along with it. "I'd love to, please."

"Very well, I'll take you up Taffy Highway to Mapo Hall — that is the Town Hall. From there you'll get a lovely view of Ibadan."

"What an odd name, Taffy Highway. Do you know why it is called that?" Cecilia's sunny nature had quickly re-asserted itself.

"Not for sure. Probably built by a Welsh engineer. It was built to connect Government House on the top of one hill, to Mapo Hall on the top of another."

"The Egba's weren't the only clever people,

were they? "

"No, the British always built in the safest and most beautiful spots. And I'm told that originally the road was lined with cassia trees to give shade to pedestrians as well as beauty to the city. It must have been quite a sight when they were all in bloom. Alas, when they built the dual carriage-way they cut down all the trees and never replaced them."

They were now driving through quiet roads, under big trees, and Cecilia could see the large houses lining the road, the lights through their un-curtained windows lighting up their drives and sometimes spilling out as far as the road.

"We're about to pass Government House on our left, then we'll soon be out of this old colonial residential area and back into the true Ibadan, as we hit Taffy Highway."

"You know you've missed your vocation, Ezeilo. You'd make a smashing guide." Cecilia smiled up at his profile, dimly discernable in the half light of the car.

"I've always taken an interest in the places that my work takes me to. In the people too. Saves one from becoming too insular. You can learn a lot." He swung the landrover round on to the double carriage way as he spoke.

"I agree absolutely. I should hate to stay on the campus all the time as I gather some of the expatriates do."

Cecilia peered out of the window again, as the pulsating life of the city crowded out on to the streets. It was a noisy, raucous city here and Cecilia found it excitingly and nostalgically alive.

The view from Mapo Hall was as fascinating as Ezeilo had promised. He had managed to park the car, and had given a young boy a 'dash' to look after it. Then they had walked through the large gates at the side of the compound to climb the steps up to the front of the building from where they would get the best view.

Cecilia was amazed at the size of the city, stretching out in all directions as far as the eye could see. They stood for quite a time looking at the sea of twinkling lights spread out before them and listening to the sounds of the city, wafted up on the breeze. Ezeilo took Cecilia's bag into his safe keeping, and holding her elbow in a firm grip, he led her across the road to the market. The smell of peeled oranges and wood smoke assailed their nostrils getting stronger as they approached the stalls. The sounds were deafening: music was blaring out from the loudspeakers of a little record shop, while others had radios turned up to full volume. Above all was the sound of humans — bargaining, arguing, or just having a friendly conversation at the tops of their voices.

"Oh, I didn't realise how I have missed the noise and bustle of home," Cecilia said as they wandered through the market for a few minutes, before

Ezeilo shephered her back to the car.

"That was really something, that view, and I loved it. Thank you so much for bringing me Ezeilo.

Cecilia turned her beaming face towards him as he put the car into gear and started to drive off. "It's made me feel more homesick for Enugu than ever," she continued.

"I come from Onitsha. Perhaps we could combine our visits to our families," Ezeilo said, as he blew his horn loudly at a couple of goats eating something in the middle of the road. They looked balefuly at the landrover before moving slowly away.

"That will be out of the question. I shall be taking Tim with me to introduce him to the family," she replied stiffly.

"Of course, forgive me, it had quite slipped my mind," Ezeilo said grimly as he brought the land-rover to a halt applying the brakes with unneccessary vigour, before turning towards her and taking her head non too gently in his two hands. "Take care my little intellectual don't try me too far," and before she was even aware of his intention, he had dropped a light kiss on her mouth, "And before you remind me that I promised to behave, that was a very sexless, pure kiss. Admit it."

Cecilia could just see in the dark interior of the landrover that his face had relaxed again into a smile. He was right, it had been the sort of kiss an uncle might give his favourite niece. So why did she feel it down to her toes. If it had had any

152

effect on her companion he was hiding it well, as he slipped out of the vehicle and came round to help her out.

It was very quiet in the part of the town they had now entered, a great contrast to Oja Oba at Mapo. Cecilia, looking around, could see that very few people lived here as the restaurant was surrounded by locked up shops. Ezeilo took her arm, helping her negotiate the storm drains in their path, and pushing the long-suffering goats out of their way, until they reached the flight of stairs which led to "The Cabin."

Chapter Seven

Inside it was like walking into another world. They were greeted very cordially by the owner of the restaurant, who obviously knew Ezeilo well. He led them over to a very modern bar where every conceivable drink could be had.

Perched on a stool, a cool tomato juice in her hand, Cecilia glanced round. The lighting was very subdued and Moorish, as the wall brackets had ornamental brass shades lit by red bulbs. On the tables, red candles stood ready. The bench seats were covered in red plush cushions, and apart from a small dance floor in the centre, the room was partitioned off into booths by dark, ornately carved, wood. Soft romantic music put the final touches to a restaurant that could match all but the most exclusive in the world. And nices of all, it was beautifully cool.

154

"Happy?" Ezeilo, whose eyes had never left her face while she looked around her, smiled gently at her. If only he could always be this nice, Cecilia thought, as she covered up her sudden shyness by helping herself from the bowl of nuts on the bar top. "Very," she answered simply and sincerely, realising as she said it how true it was. It was quite ridiculous but she couldn't remember when she had felt so utterly carefree and happy. Their eyes met and held for one heady moment and Ezeilo was the one to look away first. "I think our table should be ready by now, shall we move?" he said abruptly.

Cecilia was happy to leave the ordering to Ezeilo who knew far more about Lebanese food than she did. He ordered homus to start with, which they ate with flat, unleven bread. Then to follow he ordered roast lamb which had been marinated in olive oil and wine with a delicious combination of spices, almonds, and raisins, before being roasted. He ordered a mixed platter of vegetables and for sweet, a madly fattening, delicious halva, which he said was a speciality of the house. A bottle of ice cold dry hock to wash it all down, made it a meal fit for a king.

It had certainly lived up to its expectations and the feeling of well-being that Cecilia felt spreading through her body from her head to her toes, made her communicative when Ezeilo started skillfully drawing her out of herself. She told him things

155

about her childhood that she thought she had forgotten, unaware of how much of her own heartbreak she was exposing to him.

"But that's enough about me," she said finally, biting delicately into a piece of halva. "You haven't told me anything about yourself," she smiled at him, all barriers down.

"That's because I find you a much more facinating subject." He leant across the table and took her hand in his, his eyes glittering darkly in the candle light, his mouth set in a grim line. "You had a traumatic childhood, Lia." His eyes softened as he looked at her finely drawn face, the eyes so big and luminous in the flickering light, her mouth soft and generous, and unconsciously inviting, "but, my little intellectual that is no reason to marry for emotional security. You have boldly grasped your career with both hands, now you must do the same with your emotional life."

Cecilia did not respond angrily as she would have done earlier, but a shocked look came over her face, "Do you really think that is what I am doing?"

"Don't you?" he said looking deeply into her eyes as if to see into her very soul. But a change came over Cecilia. Her eyes hardened and she pulled her hand away.

"You wouldn't be lulling me into a receptive mood would you, with this delicious food and unaccustomed wine?" she asked suspiciously. I insist on changing the subject back to you."

Ezeilo shrugged his shoulders. "What do you want to know about my dark past?" he asked, a suspicion of a smile lurking at the corners of his strong sensual mouth.

Cecilia paused while the waiter poured out their turkish coffee from a gleaming little copper pot with a long narrow brass handle. "What happened to you to make you look on women as only playthings?"

"Do I do that? "he was openly smiling now.

"Don't laugh, I am deadly serious." There was an earnest look on her face now that had driven away the soft sensuality of a minute ago. "Your attitude to women is so appalling that I feel sure there must be a woman behind it."

"But, little Lia, I do not agree with you. I think I have as normal and reasonable an attitude towards the opposite sex as you do." His eyes glittered wickedly.

"Oh! You are the most infuriating man I have ever met," Cecilia said with feeling, banging her now empty coffee cup down on its saucer.

"That is because I upset you. Admit it, I have an effect on you that disturbs and excites you right down to your toes." "You certainly have no such thing!" Cecilia retorted vehemently. She stood up abruptly, "Excuse me for a moment, will you?"

"Running away?" Ezeilo raised one eyebrow knowingly. Cecilia walked past him without a word, to take refuge in the ladies' powder room.

When she came back there were one or two couples on the dance floor and Ezeilo, standing up as she approached, took her bag and put it down on the table. "Shall we?" But it was not a question, for not waiting for an answer, he led her on to the floor. It was the last thing that Cecilia had intended to happen, but he had been too quick for her. Before she knew it, his arm was holding her close to him. She tried to pull away, but his grip tightened as he whispered in her ear, "Scared?"

"No, I certainly am not. What on earth is there to be scared of?"

"What the closeness of my body is doing to your senses. Scared that it may lead you into an emotional entanglement that will jerk you out of that cocoon of control that you have woven so tightly round your emotions, my warm sensual intellectual."

"Oh, I do wish you wouldn't keep on calling me that." Cecilia took refuge in temper.

"Very well, I shall call you my darling instead." He moved his mouth sensually over Cecilia's ear and then gently flicked his tongue into its orifice.

"Don't you dare!" Cecilia said, but it came out weakly instead of firmly as she had intended, as her treacherous body started to tremble.

"Be quiet, my darling, and relax to the pleasurable sensations that are running as sensually through your body as they are through mine. Thaw little ice-maiden."

Cecilia felt as if she were falling down a dark tunnel, and it was a heavenly sensation, her head was spinning and her legs felt as if they would give beneath her as, taking advantage of the dark lighting, Ezeilo let his mouth cover her neck with kisses, down to her throat, making her wish that it would descend further to her hardening nipples, then it moved up again, to capture her mouth. The music stopped and the suddeness of it brought Cecilia to her senses. She pulled away taking Ezeilo unawares. Her body had been so pliant and unresisting a moment before. She walked back to the table and picked up her bag, Ezeilo close behind her.

"I'd like to leave now, please," she said mustering all the dignity she could.

"Of course," he answered blandly and called for the bill.

On the journey home Cecilia huddled into her corner keeping as far away from Ezeilo as she could. Now and again she stole a glance at his profile, but it was so stern and forbidding that each time she choked back the angry words of condemnation that rose to her lips. He had pulled up outside her block of flats before he broke the silence, putting a detaining hand on her arm as she moved to open her door.

"I'm truly sorry, Cecilia, I did intend to keep my promise, but I am only made of flesh and blood." He turned her rebelling head to face him with a firm hand. "I don't think you have any idea how attractive you are. You can turn a man's head until he had no control over himself." She looked at him scornfully. "So it's my fault, is it? That's a poor excuse, and one that I never expected to hear from you."

Something snapped inside Ezeilo and he pulled her to him with rough hands, his lips descending on hers bruising them with a savage kiss that brought the bitter taste of blood to her mouth, and tears to her eyes. Careless of any hurt he might be inflicting, Ezeilo forced her unresponsive lips apart and ravaged her mouth with his demanding tongue. Her breasts were pressed so strongly against his hard chest, that she moaned with the pain. Suddenly her struggles ceased, as his caresses lost their mindless brutality and became soft and sensual, although just as urgent. Of its own volition her mouth started to return his kisses, her arms slid round his neck, her bruised young breasts strained to press closer to his manly chest and little moans of pleasure escaped her lips.

It was Ezeilo who, controlling himself with a mighty effort, pulled away gently, holding her off with a firm hand when she would have pulled his head down to hers again. "If we don't stop now I will not be able to stop at all. I will carry you off and ravish you. I won't apologise again, Lia, but you tried me beyond endurance. Besides I wanted to convince you that you are not for Tim. He can never make you happy."

160

Cecilia, heartily ashamed of her behaviour, but at the same time bitter at his sudden rejection of her, turned on him. "I suppose I should be happier being one of the casual ladies who you use to satisfy your sexual urges. You make me sick. You don't begin to know the meaning of love," her eyes flashed woundingly.

Ezeilo flinched, but replied quietly. "Perhaps I don't, not your kind of love. I only know that I want you as I have never wanted any other woman. And I am convinced that you want me but are too pig-headed to admit it."

"For your information, Doctor Obi, I wouldn't want you if you were the last man on earth." She jumped out of the car and slammed the door.

Ezeilo's lips were pressed tightly together, his mouth a grim line across his face, the skin pulling tightly over his high cheekbones, and a nerve twitching in his jaw, as he drove away at high speed.

Cecilia, without a backward glance sped into the hallway and up the stairs. It was not until she reached the safety of her bedroom that she allowed her anger to dissolve into despair. Flinging herself full length on the bed, her body was shaken with wracking sobs, as she cried as she had not cried since she was a child.

Much later, when the tears were spent, feeling drained of all emotion but far from sleep, her mind refusing to rest, she reviewed the day's happenings a thousand times. She could not erase the pleasure that she had had from his company, nor could she deny any longer that she found him devastatingly attractive. But she told herself, over and over again that what they had between them was just lust — a low animal passion, whereas she and Tim had what really mattered; mutual respect and love. That was what lasted and made a marriage. Anyway there was no question of marriage where Ezeilo was concerned. His past history and present behaviour proved that. He was condemned out of his own mouth. "I want you," he had said — not a word about love.

Her upright nature felt utterly betrayed by her errant body and she felt she had let Tim down badly when she had responded so passionately to Ezeilo's kisses, and had silently begged for more when he had drawn away. She was so ashamed everytime she thought of it. So guilty. "Dear, dear Tim." she whispered to the empty room, "I'll make it up to you, I swear I will." But when she at last fell into an uneasy sleep, it was Ezeilo who was waiting for her at the altar in her dreams, not Tim.

Inspite of of a blinding head and puffy eyes with dark shadows under them, Cecilia was in the labs bright and early the next day, to make sure that everything was ready for the batch of green spider mites that Tim should bring from Lagos by mid-morning. With the lab assistant, who had been detailed off to work with her, she checked the incubators thoroughly. She had decided to divide the batch into three and rear them under slightly different conditions, to see which would be the best for the mass production she would have to put underway shortly, when the new factory was finished.

Segun proved to be as intelligent and efficient as Ezeilo had said when he had told her which lab assistant he had detailed off to work with her on this important project. Together they worked out a roster for an hourly check on the three incubators. At night however, in the case of a power failure he assured Cecilia that the generator would automatically be fired. All that had to be done was for it to be switched on to the ready each evening. She however insisted that they should do the hourly physical check ups until ten every evening. Other things might adversely affect the green spider mites.

At first Cecilia found Segun rather truculent and wondered if he were the kind that resented working under a woman. She sighed. She had met that kind before. It was one of the minor harassments that a woman working in a man's field had to endure and she had learnt to cope with it at an early date. Being a sensitive person, she dealt with them as gently as she could, without losing authority. She hoped it would work now as it had in the past. It took valuable time but did not, she felt, waste it. So mid-morning, she invited him back to her room for coffee, and soon he was telling her of his wives and children and how bad a time his young wife was having with her first pregnancy. By the time they went back to the labs they were firm friends.

The incubators had all reached the required temperatures when Tim walked in with the long awaited parasitoids in their special container which kept them at temperatures neccessary for their survival.

Cecilia rushed to him, and in her excitement at the safe arrival of her "babies", flung her arms round his neck and kissed him.

He pulled back, looking slightly embarrassed, "Steady on, Cecilia. Remember what Ezeilo said." He patted her on the back.

Cecilia felt chastened. He was quite right of course. She wondered briefly if it had only been her excitement at the arrival of the parasitoids that had caused her to give Tim such a warm welcome — had it not something to do with guilt as well? She shrugged her shoulders. Which ever, it had not been received with a reciprocal display from him.

But soon, all her thoughts were concentrated on getting the parasitoids safely transferred to the incubators as speedily as possible. Tim lent a hand as well as Segun, and the news of their arrival seemed to have travelled fast, for Ola arrived, sent by Ezeilo, to ask if all was well. Cecilia was heartily glad that he seemed to want to avoid her as much as she wanted to avoid him. She knew they must meet quite frequently over work and she was determined to deal coolly and firmly with him. All the same she was glad not to have to face him so soon after last night. Nor did she wish him to see her puffy eyes, and have the satisfaction of knowing that he had made her cry.

Later that evening, when she and Tim were having their usual drink on his balcony, he remarked that she looked a bit under the weather. She said it was probably too much sun out on the farm.

There was a slight constraint between them. It must be my guilty conscience making me imagine things, she thought to herself as she tried all the more to please Tim. She insisted that they ate together and cooked him an especially nice meal, and as the evening progressed he became more affectionate with her to which she responded. But she noticed that both of them avoided mentioning their weekends in any detail, although Cecilia did gather that Tim had been invited to a party at the American Embassy. On her part she told him a little about the morning on the farm and mentioned casually that she had gone swimming after, but she could not bring herself to tell him about the evening she had spent with Ezeilo. She would tell him, but not just yet.

She knew that she was going out of her way to please Tim, but strangely, she felt he was doing the same to please her.

"By the way," Cecilia said, when they had

eaten their dinner and were once again sitting on the balcony in companionable silence, enjoying the coffee that Tim had insisted on making for them, "I've been invited to the Wagner's for a drink on Friday evening. You too, if you were free, Mrs Wagner said in her note."

Tim looked a little startled, "Why me? I thought she would invite you for an all-girl-together do while Wagner is out of the country."

"Perhaps she has just invited us alone," Cecilia replied.

"Anyway, I can't go. You'll have to make my apologies for me."

"Why? Don't tell me that you have to attend a meeting out of the country?"

Tim shook his head, then giving a little laugh, said, "As a matter of fact, I was going to tell you, Lee, that the Ambassador' has asked me down to spend next weekend with them."

"Oh, I see." Cecilia had a wry smile on her face, but she smiled kindly at Tim as she spoke.

"See what?" he spoke sharply, not meeting her eyes.

"Don't look now, but your ambition is showing, darling."

"Oh, is that all," Tim smiled sheepishly.

"Well he is a big fish in his way, isn't he? You never know when he might be of use to you."

Tim leaned forward eagerly. "Exactly. Now you know why I must go, don't you?"

Cecilia nodded, running her fingers through his smooth hair," Of course, darling, but couldn't you have got an invitation for me too?"

"The question of my having a fiancée never came up. Besides I knew you wouldn't have come now that your precious parasitoids have arrived." He moved away from her caress.

Ezeilo's biting remarks of the night before had left their mark. Cecilia felt a great need to put some passion into her relationship with Tim. He had been so eager for her to live with him as man and wife when she had arrived, and now, such a short time after, he seemed to be the one drawing back. Was it because he really was a cold fish as Ezeilo had said, or had her rejection of him been the cause?

She became very warm and affectionate. "I quite understand, darling, I will give your excuses to Mrs Wagner." She kissed him fondly on the mouth and then rested her head on his chest. His arm came slowly round her and he dropped a kiss on the top of her head.

"I've been thinking Tim, about us."

"What about us?" Tim sounded almost apprehensive. Cecilia lifted her head from his chest to look seriously into his eyes, "Perhaps I was wrong to refuse to sleep with you until we were married. Everybody does it nowadays." She looked down for a moment and looking up again, met his gaze squarely. "I'm prepared to do it, Tim." He dropped

167

his eyes, and she felt him stiffen beside her, before putting her from him." No, darling, I think you were quite right. I know I was upset at first by your refusal. I thought it would cement our relationship, but I've come round to your way of thinking." He kissed her gently on the cheek before continuing. "Ours has never been that sort of relationship, has it? Other things have always been more important than sex."

"Yes, I suppose you are right. Then we carry on as were were." Cecilia could not understand why, but she felt relief flood through her veins. Perhaps, she thought, as she picked up the coffee cups and took them to the kitchen, it was that she wanted to keep her relationship with Tim as different as possible from what she felt with Ezeilo — she did not want it besmirched.

The next day, she phoned Mrs Wagner to accept her invitation, warning her that it would have to be rather a brief drink as she had to watch the incubators, but telling her that she would love to come. She gave Tim's apologies and Mrs Wagner did not seem to mind at all, as Cecilia told Tim over supper. Work was a great panacea; during the day Cecilia forgot all about her tangled emotions. Even when she met Ezeilo' it was purely as a colleague. Much to her relief, he treated her as impersonally as he had always done while on the job. Her social life had become nil, as although Segun assured her nothing could go wrong with the temperatures in the incubators, she worried over her parasitoids like a mother hen, and kept going to check them several times each evening. This, Tim accepted cheerfully, knowing how important it was to the project to keep the parasitoids healthy so that they could eventually multiply.

On the following Friday, Cecilia went to the Provost's house straight from work. After checking the incubators she went to her office. She locked the door behind her. She was taking no chances of Ezeilo disturbing her as he had when she had been kissing Tim. Taking off the white jacket she wore to the labs, she stripped down to her pants and slid a crisp cotton dress over her head. She had brought a change of clothes back with her after the lunch break, to save time. It was a pretty dress in that subtle shade of mauve that looked so well against her skin. It had no sleeves and the back was cut in a deep vee which reached right down to her waist. The front was cut very simply and demurely and gave no hint of the dramatically styled back. The skirt was pencil thin, reaching down to just below the knee, showing off Cecilia's slender legs to perfection. It had a narrow matching belt of the same material. On her feet she wore a pair of pale olive-green sandals. Her heels were still too sore to wear shoes with backs, and she carried a matching handbag. The outfit would have been severe in its simplicity had she not worn a pair of large gilt hoop earrings and a chunky gilt chain. The only mirror she had was the tiny one in her bag, so she unlocked the door and went along to the ladies toilet, where she could at least see the greater part of her ensemble in the mirror over the wash-basins. Satisfied with what she saw, Cecilia returned to lock up her office, before setting off to Mrs Wagner's.

It was Cecilia's first visit to the house provided for the Provost and his family, and she was looking forward to seeing inside it.

She left the car, which had now been put at her disposal, in the pleasant park provided at the end of the drive, and climbed the smooth white terrazzo steps to the front door. It was a large plateglass door set between two wall-to-ceiling windows. As both these and the door were curtained, she could not see into the house until the steward let her in. There was a hall area with the same beautiful shiny white terrazzo, which, Cecilia was to discover, ran right through the main rooms of the house. She stood for a moment looking around her.

"Hello my dear. How nice that you were able to come," and Mrs Wagner took her by the arm and led her down the stairs into the lounge. Cecilia gasped when she saw the view.

The lounge was large, with shaggy white rugs thrown down on the floor, while the comfortable sofas and chairs were covered in delicate pinks, browns, and greens. It looked very fresh and cool. The large coffee tables had lovely pieces of Nigerian carving or sculpture adorning them — Cecilia recognised a Fakeye and a Ben Enwonwu among them — while the lamps were tall and elegant and very American. But it was the view beyond, that had made her gasp. The very large floor space in front of her was half sitting-room, the other half being a covered veranda. It was not the ultra-modern tan leather and iron-mesh furniture on the verandah, nor the lovely local pots, that caught Cecilia's eyes as she looked past the sitting-room. It was the massive wall of bougainvillea bushes, seen through the mosquito netting that surrounded the verandah. It was a breath-taking sight; a riot of colours in a most dramatic display only about twenty yards from the house. It meant that there was no other view but it ensured privacy.

"It sure is a lovely display, I never tire of looking at it," Mrs Wagner said, and stood by the girl's side for a moment to let her enjoy it to the full. Then turning to sit down on one of the sofa s she continued, "What would you care for, my dear, tea of coffee? Or something cold?" Sitting on a chair near to her hostess, Cecilia answered with a smile, "Do you know, I think I should love a cup of tea I haven't had one for ages, and it is so beautifully cool in here."

Mrs Wagner nodded. "It is fully airconditioned of course, but do you know I hardly ever have it on, except in the bedrooms. That is my only criticism about this house. The bedrooms are all rather small. They all have bathrooms *en suite* of course, which is so convenient as we often have guests."

The steward had come to take their orders while they were talking, and in a very short space of time returned with a pot of tea and a plate piled high with assorted cookies.

"I thought you might like to sample some of our American cookies." Mrs Wagner held out the plate towards Cecilia, "You call them biscuits, I believe, like the British do."

Cecilia nodded, taking two on to her plate. "Yes, but they are never like these. I was introduced to your gorgeous home-made American ones when I stopped off to visit some friends in the States on my way to Mexico, and I found them so good that I feared for my figure. But a few months of trekking round large farms in the heat of the day soon had me slim again." Cecilia took a bite of one of her cookies.

"I'm sure you don't really have to worry about your figure. It is beautiful, and you are looking very charming this afternoon," she smiled as she added, "and not a bit like a high-powered Biological Control scientist."

"Thank you, Mrs Wagner, I know some people have set ideas as to what a female scientist should look like." There was a bitter note to Cecilia's voice, not lost on her astute hostess. "Ah! Doctor Obi has been airing his views, has he?" She lifted

172

up the teapot, "More tea, dear?" Cecilia shook her head, "No thank you, Mrs Wagner, I haven't finished this one yet. I've been too busy tucking in to the cookies. And yes, he certainly has!" She leant towards her hostess, "And I am determined that he shall change those views."

"I am sure that if anyone can make him, it will be you. As a matter of fact, when I first saw you I thought that Ezeilo had met his match."

Cecilia looked up quickly. Had there been an odd note in Mrs Wagner's voice? If there had, there was nothing showing in her calm, kindly eyes.

"And how is Tim? I'm sorry that he couldn't accompany you."

"So was I, but as I told you on the phone, he had to go to Lagos."

Mrs Wagner nodded, "He had to attend a party at the Embassy, I think you said." She looked at Cecilia for confirmation, and this time without asking, she replenished her teacup.

"Yes. Thank you." Cecilia took the cup from her hostess and put it carefully down on the table before her, as Mrs Wagner continued. "I wonder how Merribel has enjoyed her week's stay at the Embassy? The house is so quiet without her, but her father and I felt there wasn't enough for her to do here. She gets rather easily bored, you know. I think girls do at that age."

Cecilia felt a bit guilty, for truth to tell she had not asked Tim about Merribel at all. Her mind had been far too pre-occupied with work and her own emotional problems. "Of course, Tim took Merribel down with him last weekend. That's how he met the Ambassador and his wife. They very kindly asked him to stay the night and attend their party."

A look of relief swept over Mrs Wagner's face, but was gone in a flash. "So he did, I'd quite forgotten." But Cecilia was quite sure that she had not forgotten. She felt that the older woman was worried lest she should be jealous. "I expect he will bring her back with him this weekend, Mrs Wagner." Cecilia was anxious to let her hostess know that she was not the jealous kind. Mrs Wagner paused for a fraction of a second, eyeing Cecilia very seriously, almost as if she wanted to communicate something to her, then changing her mind, said, "I do hope that you didn't put off a chance of a pleasant weekend with your fiance just to have tea with an old woman like me."

Cecilia smiled, "No I didn't, Mrs Wagner. I couldn't have gone even if. . ." she stopped herself quickly. She had no wish to let the other woman know that she had not been asked. "I couldn't have gone because of my works," she amended quickly. "Tim brought me the batch of parasitoids I'd been waiting for when he came back last Monday, the batch from which I hope to eventually breed millions, enough to exterminate the green spider mite from Africa."

Looking at her closely, Mrs Wagner saw how her

face lit up at the mention of her work. "You are just as dedicated as Ezeilo, I think," she said.

For some reason that she hadn't time to analyse, Cecilia felt that a criticism of Tim was implied. "So is Tim, Mrs Wagner."

Mrs Wagner patted her hand in a motherly fashion. "Of course, my dear, of course. I meant to slight on your fiance. I am very fond of him." She changed the subject smoothly. "Now tell me, when do you two propose to tie the knot?"

Cecilia took the last sip of tea and put her cup down. "Do you know, we seem to have been too busy to name the date. But we are in no hurry, Mrs Wagner."

"Do you think that wise, my dear?" Mrs Wagner sounded anxious, "How long have you been engaged?"

"Let me see, it must be about eighteen months by now."

"My, but that is a long time."

"I know, but we both had objectives in view before marriage." Mrs Wagner looked as if she did not approve. "But I shouldn't think we will wait much longer," Cecilia added swiftly.

"I shouldn't my dear. Even if you have been shacking up together, I believe that is the expression used, it never. . ."

Cecilia, interrupted hastily. "Whatever it is called, we haven't Mrs Wagner. I know that it isn't generally frowned on any more, and lots of couples

175

do it, but it just isn't for me."

"I'm so glad, my dear. At the risk of being old-fashioned I don't approve of it. She took Cecilia's hand in the two of hers "But that makes an engagement all the more of a strain. And if the young man would rather have shacked up with his girl while waiting for marriage, that makes the strain even greater" She smiled apologetically at Cecilia. "You must forgive me for poking my nose in where it isn't wanted, I guess."

"Say anything you want, dear Mrs Wagner. I feel as if I have known you for ages." And it was true. In the space of half an hour, Cecilia felt closer to the woman sitting beside her than she had ever felt to her own mother. All the same she could not burden her with any of her own problems. Cecilia deduced that not only was Mrs Wagner genuinely concerned for herself and Tim, but there was an underlying concern for her own daughter too.

"I think I have given you more than enough advice for one day. Fancy me advising such a top scientist too! You must think I am taking liberties." She smiled at Cecilia as she released her hand saying, "once a mother always a mother, I guess."

"Thank you for your advice, Mrs Wagner, but our relationship, Tim's and mine, is founded on mutual respect and love."

"I'm glad to hear it. All the same no relationship is ever static; it grows or it declines. When you wait too long before marriage there is a real danger of decline. At that moment there was a peal on the front door bell and Mrs Wagner rose to her feet, "But with a beautiful intelligent girl like you. . ." she let the sentence tail off as she went to the door saying over her shoulder, "This should be some of the ladies who are on the committee for the arrangements for World Night."

Mrs Wagner was correct. As Cecilia also rose to her feet, glancing at her watch as she did so, in walked Nike, Megan and Mrs Shivra.

After greetings were over, Cecilia made her excuses, for although they all pressed her to stay, she wanted to do the hourly check on the incubators.

Chapter Eight

Cecilia spent a quiet weekend, writing up her notes on the progress of her work. She did emerge from her flat a couple of times, each time making sure that there was no sign of Ezeilo's car outside the building. She drove over to see how the 'factory' was progressing, and was delighted. She suspected it might be finished well before the completion date. Soon she must put the newly hatched parasitoids on to the cassava plants that Tim had been growing in the nursery for that purpose. It would be a controlled experiment of course, and it was imperative that no other insects should be allowed into that greenhouse. This was very difficult at present, but it would be easy once the factory was built, encased in it's special plastic bubble under which the air pressure would be kept higher than the pressure outside, so that in the .case of a leak, air would be unable to come in bringing with it other insects. Cecilia let her thoughts roam on as she walked slowly back from the site.

Before dinner on Saturday, she popped in to see Nike to find out more about World Night.

"I was going to come and see you to tell you," Nike said, as they sat out on the porch, a cool drink in their hands. "Each country puts on some traditional entertainment and the ladies from each country get together to cook some of their special dishes. It's quite a spread I can tell you, and the food is yummy" Cecilia laughed, "I can see your mouth watering already. I'd love to come Nike, but. . ."

"No buts, it's a must." Nike was very firm, "You'll love it. It's one of the best nights we have out here. There's dancing afterwards too. We all pay about a Naira to get in and it goes to charity."

"I'd really love to, but when did you say it was again?" Nike told her the date, and Cecilia shook her head doubtfully. "It's just about the time that I shall be rearing another generation of parasitoids from the ones that have reproduced on the cassava plants, and it's imperative that I don't lose them." She also sounded firm.

"Cecilia, there is such a thing as being too conscientious. What can go wrong?"

"Well nothing really. Every eventuality seems to have been taken care of. But if anything happens to the controlled temperatures in the incubators. . ." she said turning to Nike. "You remember that I lost a third of the original batch because the temperature of one incubator was not high enough."

Nike nodded. "But you were experimenting then, weren't you, to find the right temperature for the little dears?" Nike's flippancy towards their work, always amused Cecilia and knowing how seriously Dolapo took his job she had long since decided that it was just what he needed to prevent hypertension setting in.

"I was going to ask you to join our dance troup, but under the circumstances, I'd better let you off that." She handed a dish of nuts to Cecilia, who refusing with a smile, admonished her friend, "And neither should you, my girl."

"I know, but I have absolutely no will-power. Our hot climate can make you like that," she added dramatically. Cecilia laughed, "Come off it! The climate hasn't got you and you know it. You have the energy and determination of an Amazon. I've never seen anything like it. All the activities you cram into your day. And your children are exactly like you."

"They exhaust me!" Nike lolled back in her chair, the picture of exhaustion, and then burst out laughing. "Oh, all right, you win. I'll admit I could diet if I wanted to, but I am happy as I am."

"And very attractive as you are, "added Cecilia Sincerely.

"Do you really think so?" she was serious for a minute, a frown creasing up her wide forehead. Cecilia nodded. "Thank you. I always think that compliments from your own sex are worth much more than from men, don't you? I mean another woman can't have ulterior motives, can she?"

"I shouldn't have thought so," Cecilia smiled.

"Mind you, when a man like Ezeilo pays me compliments I positively purr, " Nike said, her mouth breaking into a grin.

"I can't think why. They wouldn't be worth the paper they were printed on, if you see what I mean. Not that he would ever be so foolish as to put anything in writing. Oh no! Not him." Cecilia spoke so derisively that her friend looked at her oddly.

"I told you once before that you have got that man all wrong. He's the salt of the earth, really he is." Nike put her empty glass down on the table between them.

"Well, I don't happen to think so," Cecilia finished her drink with a gulp and almost banged her glass down on the small table beside her. "Oh, I'll give you that he is brilliant, dedicated, and even good looking, if you like his rather obvious brand."

"But you don't?" Nike looked keenly at her friend, because I'd have sworn there was a deep attraction between you two. The air is electric when you are together."

"You're imagining things," Cecilia exclaimed vehemently.

"Am I?" Nike's voice was soft.

"Yes, you are. If there is any electricity it is

from our mutual dislike."

"They do say that hate is akin to love." Again Nike spoke softly.

"For goodness sake let's stop talking about Ezeilo Obi. It sends my blood pressure up," Cecilia said, determined to stop the discussion.

"All right," Nike replied equably, "lets talk about Tim. I haven't seen much of him for some time."

"He's fine, just the same as ever, good, calm, reliable Tim."

"And is that really all you want out of marriage — calmness and reliability? It sounds very dull to me. Not a bit what I should expect a girl like you to settle for."

"When you've had a childhood like mine, I think it is just what you require," answered Cecilia, crossing her legs and clasping her hands round her knees.

"And I think that you are over-reacting. You should take a good look at yourself in the mirror."

"I should? What on earth for?" Nike had all Cecilia's attention now.

"To look at the kind of woman you see there. Shall I tell you what you would see?" She continued without waiting for permission, "You would see a woman of determination and intelligence above the average. A woman with an extremely lovely feminine body and face that although not possessing a chocolate box beauty, when lit up with the personality within is possessed with true beauty. The beauty of the soul." Cecilia, embarrassed by such fullsomeness, made as if to speak. "No don't interrupt me, because now I am coming to the emotional propensities shown in that face. I see a woman capable of great and lasting passions, but I also see fear causing her to repress those passions with dogged determination. There, I've said it."

There was a pause. Cecilia sat gazing out into the evening sky, lost in thought. Nike anxious that she might have tried their short friendship too far, continued gently. "You may hit me if you wish, but I had to say it." Cecilia turned her head slowly towards Nike, then her lovely mouth quivered into a smile. "I'm not offended, just overwhelmed by your flattering description of what I should see in the mirror — until the last bit that is. That I think has rather shattered me."

"Think about it. And be very very sure that Tim really is the right man for you."

"Tim is . . . ." Cecilia rushed to his defence, but Nike interrupted her with a smile, "I know, Tim is a dear, and I am very fond of him, but I am not sure that he is right for you."

"You're not?" Cecilia looked at her friend wide-eyed. Nike shook her head, "My guess is that the things that brought you together were propinquity and a shared interest. Then for you, the lack of passion between you made you feel safe." She looked shrewdly at Cecilia. "Am I right, about the lack of passion?" Cecilia nodded reluctanly, "and for Tim part of your attraction was that he thought with your brains you would be an asset in the furtherance of his career."

"That last is a bit harsh," said Cecilia who was being forced to face reality for the first time, and found it hurt, down to the centre of her being. But even so she still sprang to Tim's defence.

"I don't mean it nastily, I don't think he is that calculating, it's more of an instinct with him." Nike looked at Cecilia, and seeing the doubts and fears that she had deliberately aroused tensing her friend's face and making her eyes deep pools of distress, took her hand warmly in her own. "I'm so sorry to have upset you. I just don't want you to make a mistake that you will regret for the rest of your life."

Cecilia gave her a wry smile. "You're the second person to try to make me think about my relationship with Tim. Mrs Wagner did it too. In the nicest way of course, and she didn't come on as strongly as you, but then she's not my best friend like you are."

"No, but she is Merribel's mother." Cecilia smiled, "And Merribel is in love with Tim."

"Exactly," her friend replied.

There was another pause, both girls busy with their own thoughts. Then Cecilia muttered, "I wonder... I wonder."

"Wonder what?"

Cecilia shook her head. She wasn't prepared to share that thought, not even with Nike, "Nothing, it was nothing."

"Auntie Cecilia! Auntie Cecilia!" Seyi's voice cried out from an upstairs window, "Aren't you ever going to come and read to us? You promised, and Bisi is getting very sleepy." Nike grinned, "That means he is. You don't have to you know. I'll tell them that you aren't feeling well." Nike rose to her feet. But Cecilia was already on hers. "I wouldn't dream of disappointing them. Promises must be kept." She smiled rather grimly. "Those you make to children at any rate. Don't worry, it will do me good." She paused a minute before entering the house. "Thanks Nike, you're a very good friend." But there was a glint of tears in her eyes. Then she went into the house shouting, "I'm coming kids, I'm coming."

And you, Nike thought, watching the receding back of her friend running lithely up the stairs, are a grand person.

Cecilia got very little sleep that night. The more she thought over what Nike had said, and Mrs Wagner too, the more she realised that she had been prepared to settle for frienship instead of love. Suddenly Ezeilo's words sprang to mind, "You have boldly grasped your career with both hands, you must do the same with your emotional life." He had been telling her the same thing.

Determinedly pushing aside all thoughts of Ezeilo,

and the fact that he made her heart pound and her pulses race faster than they had ever done before, she spent the still silent hours of the night thinking deeply about herself and Tim. She finally came to the conclusion that the good warm relationship she and Tim had had together wasn't enough for her. Not if she were honest. If she were honest, she now knew that she needed much more than that from a relationship. She must have the courage to take the risk of being hurt, before the right man came along. Meanwhile she had her work to occupy her mind and the hours of the day.

Cecilia felt as if an immense weight had been lifted off her shoulders. A weight that she had not realised that she had been carrying. She found that she was thirsty and felt like a cup of tea, so she slipped on her pale pink kimono and padded barefoot to the kitchen. While the kettle was boiling, her thoughts turned to Merribel. At Nike's she had wondered if Tim were already in love with Merribel. Poor Tim if it were so, valiantly trying to hide his feelings and keep faith with her. The more Cecilia considered his behaviour since her arrival, the more she thought that Tim had fallen for Merribel. The way he had tried to make her live with him. That was not like Tim. He must have been trying desperately to make a go of it with her. Cecilia had not a jot of self-pity in her make-up; instead her tender heart went out to Tim. Poor Tim, how he must have suffered, and Merribel.

Taking her cup of tea back to bed, Cecilia determined to speak to Tim at the earliest possible moment.

But by the time she fell into a troubled sleep, Cecilia's pillow was wet with tears.

However, seven o'clock the next morning found her checking the incubators and the young parasitoids on the cassava bushes in the controlled greenhouse, as she usually did. She looked neat and feminine, and if she had dark shadows under her slightly swollen eyes, there was such a brisk determined air about her that no one would have dared to comment on them.

It wasn't until mid-morning that she had a chance to talk to Tim. At first he tried to protest when she told him the conclusions she had come to about their relationship. But in the end, looking relieved, he told her everything.

"I didn't want to hurt you. I never meant it to happen," he explained, the words falling over themselves as they poured out. "At first I spent time with Merribel because she was the Provost's daughter as I told you, but then," he blushed, looking embarrassed, "well, it just happened. For her too. I told her that it was no use, that I had a fiancée. She accepted that and said that we should live from day to day. Then you arrived, he looked sheepish again, "and it was awful for her."

"I'm sure it was," Cecilia spoke sympathetically, "but you should have told me."

"I know I should. I just didn't have the courage, I suppose." He looked down, ashamed.

"It's lucky that I had. We would all have been hurt much more you know, if you and I had married."

There was a pause, then rather hesitantly Tim said, "As a good friend, which I hope I will always be, Cecilia, may I ask you a personal question?"

"Of course you may. I too hope that we will always be good friends," Cecilia answered readily.

"Has Ezeilo anything to do with your decision?" Cecilia flared up at once, "For heavens sake, no! I can't stand the man. Why does everyone think that he is so irresistible to women? He's not my type at all. You should know me better than that! I like a serious type of man."

"But he is a serious type and. . ."

Cecilia picked up her white jacket from where she had placed it over a chair, and started to move to the door of her office, "There's one thing," she said with a wry smile at Tim, "he won't get another chance to reprimand us like school children for kissing in the office." They grinned at each other and the atmosphere lightened between them. Cecilia continued, her hand on the door, "He'll be very pleased not to have an engaged female on his staff anymore, but he is sure to expect increased efficiency. "A bitter note had crept into her voice as she spoke. Then turning slowly to look back at Tim, she said, "Do me a favour, would you?"

"Of course, anything, you know that." Tim's voice was warm with affection.

"Can we keep quiet about our break-up for a week or two?" It had suddenly occured to her as she had mentioned Ezeilo's name, what harassment she might have to endure from him if he knew her engagement to Tim was off. She felt she simply couldn't take it at the moment.

"Of course, take as long as you want." Tim followed her to the door and Cecilia put her hand on his arm, "Thanks, Tim," she had the door half open when she turned back to him once more, smiling, "Of course you must tell Merribel, but swear her to secrecy."

"I'll do that, never fear," Tim replied, as they made their way back to the labs.

Cecilia worked hard and long during the next few days, in a deliberate effort to make herself so tired that she just fell asleep as soon as her head touched the pillow. Her scars healed more quickly than she had expected. Luckily possessing no false pride made Tim's rejection of her far another easier to bear; besides, she had not been in love with him, she realised that, so she had no reason to feel jilted. Her naturally optimistic nature re-asserted itself a little more each day. So when Nike reminded her of World Night, saying that she and Dolapo always made up a table and of course expected her and Tim to join them, she began to look forward to it with pleasure.

Tim said Merribel was most understanding, and didn't mind his accompanying Cecilia this last time, so it was settled. Her only problem was the hourly checks that she had been making on the incubators every evening. The parasitoids multiplied rapidly, but she was still anxious to keep a batch of each fresh generation in the incubators, incase anything drastic should kill off those in the green-house. The only possible person that she could trust to help her was Segun. Luckily when she approached him he was very willing to help.

"Of course, Doctor Onochie, I will do the checks for you," he said. "I live very close to the campus, it will be no trouble to me. We are having a naming ceremony and small party — my junior wife has been safely delivered of a baby boy," he said smiling from ear to ear.

"I'm so glad for you, she was having a bad time with the pregnancy wasn't she?"

"Yes, so I am very relieved."

"And pleased that it is a boy too. But in that case. . ." Segun interrupted her, "It will be quite all right. I shall be able to do it, all the guests will have gone by then."

"If you're sure?" He nodded. "Then thank you, Segun. It will only be the nine p.m. and the ten p.m. ones. I can do the eight myself." She smiled at Segun, I am most grateful, for there is no one else I would trust." Segun looked very pleased. There was no sign at all of his earlier truculence.

When Cecilia arrived at the party, she gasped at the sight that met her eyes: the women had done a terrific job, with some carpentry assistance from the more handy husbands. The hall was completely transformed. Standing just inside the entrance there was a larger than life plywood figure of an Indian in a splendid bejewelled turban, his hands raised palm together in the traditional Indian greeting. Flying right across the width of the hall was a magnificent paper dragon in reds, pinks and gold.

Spaces along the walls had been alloted to the various countries and each had tried to out do the others with their decorations. The Swiss had a large blow up of a snow-covered mountain as back ground, and a picture of a lovely fat, fawn cow with a large cow-bell round it's neck stood in front of it; there was a display of fine lace and wood carvings, and on the opposite side was another cut-out of a large brown bear standing up on its hind legs. The Indians had the Taj Mahal as their centre piece and the sides were draped with beautiful saris in every imaginable colour, richly woven, some with gold thread others with silver.

The Japanese had made a miniature garden round a pagoda. The Indonesians had a display of shadow puppets — that they would use later. The Dutch, predictably, used a windmill as their centre-piece, while the British had large blown up photos of the Prince and Princess of Wales with Her

191

Majesty the Queen in between them and the Union Jack flew over their heads.

Cecilia, who had been far too busy to help, was delighted with the Nigerian display: the background was draped with lovely cloths pieces from all over Nigeria, and the centre piece was a large blow-up of the famous Benin Bronze head. It was draped with the National flag and tastefully surrounded by wood carvings and traditional pots. On one of the display tables was a complete little Northern village carved out of thorn. It even had a little school house and a forge.

Cecilia simply couldn't take it all in. There were so many people admiring the decorations that it was not easy to see them all clearly.

Tim helped them both to a glass of punch from a tray that appeared at their elbow. He was putting himself out to be nice to her, and ironically, as Cecilia was quick to notice, paying her more compliments than he had ever done. She did not realise how deserving of them she was. She was wearing her favourite evening dress, a pure white silk jersey affair off one shoulder in Grecian style, and falling to the ground in heavy folds. She had, however, nipped the waist in with a gold belt and wore her gold strappy sandals. It's classic beauty showed to perfection her lovely slender body, clinging to every feminine curve. Save for a pair of small gold hoops in her ears, she wore no jewelry, realising that the dress was perfection in itself. As

192

usual she wore little make-up, just enough to accentuate her large brown eyes which were sparkling with anticipation of the evening ahead.

She intended to enjoy her evening off to the full, and didn't mean to let anything spoil it, not even the presence of Ezeilo Obi. Nike had warned her in advance that he was always a member of their party, so she knew he would be sitting at their table. He was not likely to bring a companion; it wasn't neccessary at these affairs, Nike had told her. Well, she would cope with Doctor Obi coolly and decisively. All the same she was glad she still had her engagement to Tim to hide behind.

By the time Tim found their table, Megan and Charles were already there, having forgone their beloved hang-gliding in order to attend. Cecilia was pleased, for a warm friendship was springing up between her and Megan. They greeted each other gaily, and while the men went for more drinks, Cecilia insisting on something soft, they chatted about this and that.

"Look," Megan said suddenly. "There are the Wagners coming in now. And just look at Merribel! Why I haven't seen her sparkling like that for a long time." Cecilia made no comment but she saw that Megan was right. Gone was the rather sullen girl that she had first met Merribel seemed to have blossomed into a woman overnight. Tim and Charles on their way back from the bar stopped to greet the Wagners, and Cecilia could see the love shining out of Merribel's eyes as she smiled up at Tim. For a moment she felt a little twinge of sadness, but it was gone in a flash, for her armour was on tonight and she too was sparkling, putting Merribel in the shade, had she but realised it.

Nike and Dolapo arrived as Tim brought the drinks to the table, so the three men went back to the bar again to fetch more drinks, while the three girls sat looking round at the assembled gathering, discussing the outfits of the other women. It was a light-hearted discussion for none of them was obsessed by clothes, Megan least of all, much preferring to be in old jeans and a T-shirt all day.

"There are some lovely dressed here, aren't there Megan? But I think that our Cecilia will be the belle of this ball," Nike said after a while.

"I couldn't agree with you more," said a deeply masculine voice behind Cecilia's shoulders; a voice that held a teasing quality behind the sincerity of the words. "She looks quite breath-takingly beautiful, all in white." Cecilia stiffend. She was sure he was taunting her. Then she felt a light kiss on the top of her head. "I'm sure Tim won't mind my giving you such a chaste kiss," Ezeilo said softly.

"Not at all, old man," said Tim cheerfully, putting a large chapman down in front of Nike. "Looks as if we're going to have a good crowd here tonight," he continued looking round the room, as he sat next to Cecilia.

194

"It does, doesn't it," agreed Ezeilo, as he took the seat on the other side of her.

It certainly did. The tables, all for eight or ten people, were fast filling up and the stewards were hovering round for orders for wines with the meal. "I think champagne is called for, don't you, Cecilia?" Ezeilo had an odd glitter in his eyes.

"It's a banned import, isn't it?" she replied coolly.

"My, my, we are getting up to date fast!" Ezeilo's left eyebrow was raised. It annoyed Cecilia intensely.

"Not at all, Nike told me," was her sharp reply.

"Having been back home considerably longer than you, Lia," he went on, unperturbed by her asperity, "I'm afraid I was referring to the Nigerian champagne, made from Kola nuts. Not quite as good I know, but it is quite plentiful, and . . . . " Ezeilo's voice trailed off as he waved to a steward. "I take it that everyone is happy with the choice?" He addressed the table, which Butch and the Shivras had now joined.

"High-handed as usual," Cecilia said bitingly. Ezeilo gave a hearty laugh, "If you like to call it that. Just making the party go with a swing, I should call it." Cecilia could have hit him. The arrogance of man! "I was under the impression that this was Nike and Dolapo's table," she said, between clenched teeth.

He nodded amicably, "So what?" he went serious for a moment, " and I happen to owe them a lot of hospitality, Lia. If I hadn't done it in the manner in which I did, Dolapo would have felt the onus was on him to provide wine for the table." He glanced down at her and found that even sitting down, he towered over her. He tweaked a bouncing curl at her ear and whispered, "I hope you don't jump to such illogical conclusions in your work, my little intellectual, without first ascertaining the facts."

Cecilia was furious at having put herself in the wrong. She had jumped to conclusions. But she was equally furious with him for baiting her. "I think that by now you know me better than that." She was icily angry.

He gave her a little mocking bow. As always, his mere physical presence was totally un-nerving her. That and the familiar scent of him, mixed with the hauting fragrance of his after-shave, aroused all her sensuality that had lain dormant for so long. She knew that she was taking defence in anger, knew that he was aware of the confusion he caused to her usually so calm and collected self. And she knew he revelled in it in the most devilish manner. He was playing with her like a cat with a mouse, and they both knew it. Cecilia deliberately turning her back on him, greeted Mrs Shivra, who was sitting on the other side of Tim.

"Please call me Beela," Mrs Shivra responded warmly," and I may call you, Cecilia, isn't it?"

"Please do, Beela." Cecilia couldn't believe that

Mrs Shivra would be so approachable; she was so grand. She was certainly looking very grand tonight. She was not wearing a sari, and when Cecilia questioned her about it, saying how much she admired the full, swirling skirt and long blouse top, Beela explained that it was her Rajasthan costume. It was heavy with gold embroidery and she was bedecked with jewellry, which she said had been handed down from one generation to another. She wore the most ornate nose decoration that Cecilia had ever seen: it was attached to her nose and hung in a loop across her cheek to where it was fastened round her ear. It was solid gold, patterned richly in green, red, and white enamel with a little fringe of fresh-water pearls. She wore matching earrings. But Cecilia couldn't help feeling that it must be rather awkward, not to say painful carrying all that weight on her ear and nose. But on looking round other tables she noticed that all the Eastern women were richly and ornately dressed in their native costumes. She did notice however, that the other Indian women were wearing saris and no one had such gorgeous jewelry as Beela. As she was happy to explain to Cecilia, the women must adorn themselves as a compliment to their husbands.

The food was all that Nike had said it would be. Before Cecilia was halfway round the buffet table her plate was filled with unknown delicacies that she wanted to taste. And the aroma that drifted up her nostrils stimulated her appetite.

"I have no intention of worrying about my figure," Nike announced firmly, as she helped herself liberally to everything. Megan and Cecilia laughed.

"It's all right for you two thin things. You can pile your plates sky-high and nobody would think that you were greedy, but if you are plump like me, people immediately think, what a greedy pig, even when you do not have half as much on your plate. You can see it in their eyes."

Again her friends laughed.

"But this time, love," Cecilia said, "you have got a lot on your plate."

A little smug smile played around Nike's mouth for a moment, as she helped herself to yet another delicacy. "I wasn't going to tell you just yet, but I can't keep it a secret much longer, so I may as well — I happen to be eating for two." She beamed at her friends on either side of her in the queue.

"Nike!" Cecilia exclaimed in delight.

"Then do you think you should be eating all this spicy food?" said Megan who with a wink at Cecilia, put a hand on Nike's plate.

"Oh no you don't, hands off! I intend to produce a very cosmopolitan baby," said Nike, holding on firmly to her plate.

"You girls seem to be enjoying yourselves," Charles remarked on their return to the table. "Come on you guys it's our turn now, but by the looks of things we'll be lucky if the women have left us a few crumbs." But when they came back their plates were piled even higher!

Cecilia found that much as she would have liked to finish the food on her plate she was quite unable to although compared with the others she had taken a modest amount. She suddenly felt nervous and on edge. In her heart she knew the cause — the infuriating, macho man sitting beside her, looking so handsome in dark slim evening trousers and ruffled white evening shirt, worn tonight, as it was at gala night, with a black silk bow tie and a black silk cumberbund, the latter, tightly fastened round his slim waist emphasising the breadth of his massive chest and shoulders. Cecilia was not a short girl by any means, but she felt positively dwarfed beside him and found it intimidating.

Noticing that she could not eat her food, he whispered in her ear, "Off your food I see. Must be love." Pushing his own plate away he was on his feet in one swift movement and pulling her to hers. "Come and dance," he turned to Tim. "You don't mind if I dance with your fiance, do you?" he asked, taking the answer for granted, as he swept Cecilia away to the dance floor where a few other couples were already dancing to the excellent band provided.

"As arrogant as usual," Cecilia said coldly, as he swept her into his arms. Luck is always with him, she thought. He always gets a slow. If only the tempo was fast he would have no excuse to hold me at all. But it wasn't, and short of creating a scene she had to allow him to put his arm round her and hold her closely to him. She wasn't going to struggle, she remembered that that had only made matters worse the last time.

"You are looking lovelier than ever, darling intellectual, but did I detect the signs of tears around your eyes last week?"

Damn the man for being so observant! she thought. Their paths had crossed on very few occasions since that fateful Saturday, she had seen to that, and still he had noticed. "Too much sun makes my eyes swell," she replied coolly.

"And gives you shadows under them as well?" he questioned softly as he started to kiss her ear.

"Stop it, Ezeilo!" Cecilia could feel the blood rushing up to the roots of her hair, and what was worse, her bones were melting, as delicious tremors went through her at his caress." Behave properly or I shall walk off the floor." She pulled her head away, while she still had the strength to do so.

"Relax darling, stop fighting it. We are meant to enjoy each other so. . ."

"Is that all you ever think about, enjoyment? I've told you before I am not that sort of girl," Cecilia's flashing brown eyes met a pair glittering with humour, and showing a determination that sent little shivers of fear along her sensitive nerves.

"You'll lose if you try to fight it, so why not enjoy it. Deny if you can that you want me as

200

much as I want you." He held her closer until she could feel his aroused masculinity. Her body went pliant, but her mind and spirit still fought on.

"I do not!" she denied vehemently, her lovely breasts rising and falling rapidly against his chest, her eyes flashing fire.

"It's naughty to tell lies little Lia. Look at me." There was such authority in his voice that she instinctively obeyed, but with eyes still passionately alight with anger. They were caught in his intense gaze, like flies in a spider's web. They were caught, held — and she was lost. For she felt the anger die out of her and another emotion take its place. With a shock, she realised that she loved this man! This man who only wanted her for his pleasure, to play with and then to throw away, as he must have done with all the others.

Time stood still. Then with a moan of pain, Cecilia tried to pull her body away from his, "Let me go!" she whispered fiercely.

Ezeilo at once released his hold, "For the moment. But I warn you, Lia, I shall do everything in my power to prove to you that Tim is not the man for you."

"And you are, I suppose?" she sneered. Her voice was icy cold again, her body stiff. Try as she might, she could not control its trembling. "I'd like to go back to the table."

He gave her a mocking little bow, "Your wish is my command," he said, but there was still a look of determination in his eyes that made her shiver.

For the rest of the evening Cecilia was in a daze, her emotions running riot. The realisation that she was in love with Ezeilo shocked her. But it also filled her with a wild joy, marred only by the knowledge that he did not love her. He just wanted her physically. He had made that quite clear all along. Only her observant friend, Nike, noticed the turmoil she was going through. So well did she hide it from those around her.

Ezeilo left her strictly alone, dancing with the other women at the table, talking and laughing with the men. Cecilia danced with Tim and then sent him to dance with Merribel who came back to their table for a while, her gratitude to Cecilia showing in the warmth with which she greeted her.

The floor show started and though it was marvellous, Cecilia could not remember a thing about it afterwards. Not even how fetching Nike looked dancing her Tiv dance, nor how gracefully Beela had danced the intricate Rajasthan dance with the other Indian women she had taught. Even the rather dangerous log dance by the Koreans, escaped her memory. Long after Nike told her that she had been the life and soul of the party, and when Charles had suggested that they round off the evening with a coffee, she had suggested gaily that as her place was near, why didn't they all come with her.

She realised afterwards that she must have been

on a desperate sort of high. Not from the wine, for she had been careful to have only one glass, but from emotions that had been pent up for years, topped by the bitter knowledge that this love now was unrequited.

She vaguely remembered that Nike looking at her anxiously, had protested, but had been cried down by the others. So they had all piled into their cars and driven round to her apartment.

She must have made the coffee, for she remembered pouring it out, and then gradually her friends left until only Tim and Ezeilo remained. She began to feel frightened then, so taking Tim into the kitchen on some pretext, she whispered to him that he was not to leave her alone with Ezeilo. He looked at her musingly. "Are you sure that is what you really want?" he questioned gently. She nodded her head vigourously. "I don't think that I am convinced." Tim kissed her gently. "No, I'm not convinced at all." He left her putting more water in the coffee pot.

When she returned to the living room, only Ezeilo remained, lounging casually on the sofa, looking as if he belonged there.

Cecilia turned and took the coffee pot straight back to the kitchen, furious with Tim for letting her down. Then she walked resolutely back into the room, saying stiffly, "I'm sorry, I thought Tim was here."

"He said he was tired and was off to bed," and

looking at her keenly, he added, "He went downstairs to his own flat. Does that mean that you two are no longer sleeping together? Is that what the tears were about, my little Lia?" There was no sympathy in his voice. He sounded exultant.

"I have already told you, there were no tears. Besides it is none of your business. I should like you to go now," she said firmly, but as he made no move and continued to sit there undressing her with his eyes, her spirits faltered and her voice pleaded with him as she added, "Please. . . ."

Chapter Nine

There was silence in the room, save for the constant shrill of the cicadas. Once more time stood still, as Ezeilo looked into Cecilia's pleading eyes. For an instant it felt to her as if their very souls were touching, then his mouth tightened into a determined line as his arm snaked out and Cecilia felt her wrist caught in a vice-like grip. "If I were your fiancé, I would never leave you alone with another man as he has left you. That should be enough to convince you that he is not the. . ."

"He . ." she tried to interrupt, but she was savagely drawn against him and cruel fingers fastened in her curls, forcing her head back, as Ezeilo ruthlessly cut in. "Don't interrupt me when I am speaking." His face was close to hers now, and she fought to free herself as if her life depended on it. His arrogant behaviour had sent her temper flaring, giving her the courage to defy him.

"Let go of me, you fiend! How dare you speak

to me like that!" She twisted and turned, tearing her hair and bruising her delicate wrist, as she spat the words at him.

"That will get you nowhere, my little fire brand. But already you are learning your lesson. Has Tim ever roused such passion in your breast? Let go, my little intellectual, let all that fiery passion take hold of you: lose that control over your emotions that you are so proud of." he said, holding her effortlessly against him, "and I will turn it into burning desire." He brought his mouth down so cruelly on Cecilia's soft lips, that a little cry of pain escaped her. Tears stung behind her eyes from the pain he was so heartlessly inflicting with his hands and mouth. She fought him with all her might and main. Hurt all the more by his brutal attack on her, because she loved him. The tears began to roll unheeded down her cheeks as he once more forced her lips open and plunged his tongue into the sweet cavity of her mouth. But still she fought. This was a primitive attack by an aroused male animal. Not only did it assault her body, it assaulted her spirit as well.

But the fight went out of her as her soul was filled with utter despair to think that the man she loved should take her in such a way — without one iota of love.

As if he sensed her agony of mind, he groaned and muttered against her bruised lips, "Oh, my darling, why do you drive me insane with your refusal of me? How can you cling to Tim when he is so wrong for you?" He kissed away her tears and then his mouth sought hers again, but this time with a gentleness that melted the ice round Cecilia's heart. Her sensitive loving soul could no longer hold back its love for this enigma of a man, part brute, part dove, who held her so close to his breast. Her feelings rose to engulf her like a tidal wave. At last the restraint she had been exercising so long gave way and as their kiss deepened, her arms wrapped round his neck and her mouth started to return his kisses with total abandon. Eventually his mouth moved down to rain kisses on her throat as with trembling hands he undid her gold belt and slid her dress down to her feet. Then he cupped her bare breasts in his hands and with such tender fingers, started to caress her nipples, sending sensations of wild delight straight to the core of her femininity, such delight as she had never experienced before. Then, after gazing into the velvety depth of her brown eyes, now as black as night the pupils dilated by the excitement coursing wildly through her body, he brought his lips down to first one hard nipple then the other, while Cecilia moaned with delight, twining her fingers in his thick hair. Then, as she felt his hand slip slowly down to her hips in sensual caress to find its way under her tiny froth of panties, her knees gave beneath her and she would have fallen had he not picked her up in his arms. Leaving her dress a white pool on the floor, he strode into the bedroom and placed her gently on the bed.

A glimmer of sanity came to Cecilia and she made one last effort to save herself from a fate she knew she could not resist much longer. "Please, I beg you Ezeilo," she whispered through bruised lips, as she watched him pull his shirt out of his trousers and fling it on the floor, "Tim and I didn't . . ." But she got no further, and shrank back into the pillows at the wild look of desire on Ezeilo s' face, as he un-zipped his trousers and stood naked before her.

"The only thing that would stop me from taking you now would be if you were a virgin. But that can't be, not in this day and age. Even cold-blooded Tim must have slept with you now and then," Ezeilo said, as he slipped onto the bed beside her. "Nothing else you can tell me about you and Tim can stop me. I am determined to make you mine, my darling Lia." He was all gentleness again, but he had stopped her mouth with kisses and by the time he took his lips from hers to smother her body in caresses, she no longer had the will to stop him. The blood was running as hotly through her veins as through his, as together they reached fever pitch in their desire. Cecilia was shamelessly arching her body and thrusting it against his, moaning with delight as she did so, begging him to plunder her most secret places with his roused masculinity. With a groan he mounted her, "I can wait no longer my love, I must take you now — now!" His voice was thick with passion and breathlessly she cried, "Yes! Yes please, darling — now! "as he plunged inside her a cry of pain escaped her lips, for a second Ezeilo stopped thrusting deep inside her, then he moaned, "Oh my little love, I'm sorry, but I can't stop now." Neither did Cecilia want him to. After the initial pain, she hardly felt it as it was lost in the pleasure swamping her body. Pleasure passing all her imaginings suffused her body. Then she felt her spirits rise on the wings of her physical pleasure, transporting her to higher joys that the body alone could encompass. This then was love! When they climaxed together, Cecilia felt herself swooning with ecstacy.

They lay together quietly, in perfect harmony, very slowly returning to the world. Then Ezeilo kissed her gently, looking into her eyes sorrowfully. "I'm so sorry, my lovely Lia, but I didn't think it possible that you were still a virgin."

"I was trying to tell you, " she whispered, suddenly shy now that all passion was spent.

"What a brute you must think me," he said brushing her tousled curls tenderly from her face. "I..."

"Shush! Shush! It's all right darling," she interrupted, kissing his lips tenderly.

"And I made you betray Tim. I'm sorry but I had to make you realise that he wasn't right for you." Cecilia smiled at him, her eyes enormous in her face, a face made ravishingly beautiful by love. "Tim and I broke off our engagement last week, only. . . "

A shocked Ezeilc interrupted her, "So I have been preaching to the converted? Why didn't you tell me?"

She nodded sleepily, "I did try to tell you, but you told me to keep quiet." There was a glint of a smile in her eyes. "I'm sorry, darling, but I don't think I can keep awake a moment longer."

Ezeilo slid gently from the bed, "Go to sleep, my darling, sleep well. I'll see you soon. I think it is better if I'm not found here in the morning. Not that I think Tim will mind, he must have left us together on purpose. "

But Cecilia didn't answer — she was fast asleep.

She was woken from a deep and peaceful sleep by her alarm clock shrilling in her ear. She stirred langourously at first, and then sat up with a start, as memories of the night before came flooding back to her, and the enormity of what had happened struck her. She had done the very thing that she had been determined not to do — given herself to a man who did not love her. Her heart argued that he must love her; all those sweet endearments that he had whispered last night, the beauty of their union. Surely it must have been a union of spirit as well as body? But Cecilia's head was determined not to listen. Reason told her that he had never said those all important words, "I love you," nor had he mentioned marriage. Well at least, she thought, as she dragged herself out of bed, she had given herself out of love. But how could she have been so mad as to do it? The memory of his first cruel assault on her, further persuaded her that he did not love her. His little tendernesses later no doubt were due to the fact that he was obviously a practised lover.

Once in the kitchen, she found that she was ravenously hungry, so she heated up some yam and stew left over from the day before. She felt terribly ashamed of herself. What must Ezeilo think of her now? Now that he had had her, and had the satisfaction of knowing that he was the all powerful lover, he'd probably think no more about her, she thought bitterly.

She ate the food without noticing it, lost in her thoughts, and though it satisfied her hunger, it did nothing to ease her bitter sorrow. She rose and put the dirty crockery in the sink and started to wash up out of force of habit. Then she went for her shower, which she took cold. This revived her body somewhat, but not her heavy heart. How marvellous I would have been feeling, if he really loved me, she thought unhappily, slipping into her usual jeans and T-shirt. She was beyond tears, as she thought of the days and weeks ahead when she would have to face Ezeilo. Then and there she determined not to give him a chance to refer to the incident of the night before. That way, at least, she

could prevent further heart break and embarrassment. She would be cool, business-like, and remote
with him from now on. Nothing he could do or say
would shift her from her resolve.

When she left for work, her face still bore the
signs of a woman who has had her first experience
of loving. On top of this she tried hard to impose a
cold mask.

On arriving at her office just before seven, she was
about to start her usual checks. When she noticed a
memo from Ezeilo on her desk. Her heart fluttered
in her breast and then she steadied herself as she
read it. He wanted to see her at once did he? Well,
he was the boss. if she had been expecting a love
letter, she would have been bitterly disappointed
for the memo merely said, "Come to my office the
minute you get in," signed with his usual signature,
E. O.

Cecilia put on her white jacket intending to go
straight on to the labs. Then, head held high, an
iron control on her emotions, she walked down the
corridor to his office. There was no Ola in the outer
office, so she walked through and first knocking
on the door, walked in to Ezeilo's office.

"Good morning," she started coolly, then, on
forcing herself to look him in the face with a
mighty effort, she was shocked at what she was
there. His face was an even colder mask than her
own, and what was more, it was coldy angry.

"Good morning," he returned, his voice like ice.

The qualities that she had seen a hint of on the plane, were out in full force: his mouth was set straight and the contours of his rugged face were harsh and unrelenting. He bore no resemblance to the man of the night before, and for a moment Cecilia wondered if she had dreamt it all.

There was certainly nothing lover-like about him as he took her arm in a firm grip and led her out of his office and down the passage that led to the labs. Cecilia was too shattered to speak, and he obviously had no intention of doing so, until turning into the culture room where the incubators were kept, he said in his coldly furious voice, "Take a look at number three and tell me what you see."

She did as she was bid. She opened the doors and removed the tray. She didn't need a microscope to tell that they were all dead. She turned to Ezeilo, her face shocked, "But I don't understand? What has happened? They were fine when I last checked them yesterday night."

"Exactly. I don't doubt it. But surely, even a young woman on her way to enjoy herself for the evening, if she is any kind of scientist at all, will ensure that she has shut the incubator properly."

"But I. . ." Cecilia stopped, remembering that Segun had checked after her. He must have left the doors open.

"You were about to say?" Ezeilo's voice was that of a stranger.

"Nothing," replied Cecilia dully. Better that she

should bear the brunt of his wrath, for surely if he knew it were his chief lab. assistant, he would fire him. And it was not like Segun. He had always been so dependable. She looked up at Ezeilo and even her spirit quailed, but she bravely met his eyes. "I'm sorry. It won't happen again, I can assure you. I have been keeping such a careful watch up until now. You can see from my notes. And I shall be again."

"If I give you the chance," he said haughtily. His steely eyes bore into hers. She refused to look away. Her head went up and a little fire came back into her eyes, "You cannot have me removed because of one slip, and besides, because of the way that I have organised the breeding program I shall have a fresh batch in the incubator within the next half hour." She walked past him to the door, then turning, said coldly, "At least it didn't happen because I am emotionally involved with one of your staff." There was a bitterness in her voice.

A corner of his mouth turned up sardonically, "Perhaps it was because you still wanted to be."

After what had happened between them the night before, his last remark was too much for her to bear. She walked straight back to him and dealt him a stinging blow across the cheek.

"I don't have to take that from anyone, least of all you," she said, looking at him with as much hate in her face as she had looked at him the night before with love. "I'll hand in my resignation tomorrow — Sir," and she turned on her heel and walked out.

Ezeilo looked after her with tortured eyes.

Back in her office, putting all thought of her personal worries out of mind, she first wrote out her letter of resignation. She would deliver it later when Ola would be in the office. Her next important job was to get some more larvae for the cultures. Then, she thought grimly to herself, she would find Segun.

But as it happened, Segun was in the control greenhouse checking the humidity when she appeared. She told him then and there what had happened, but cutting short his protestations, she told him that she would see him in her office in half an hour. It was a very unhappy man who left her busy getting her new larvae.

At first she did not tell Segun that she had taken the blame for his carelessness. It would do him good to sweat a bit. He had protested that he had left everything as it should be. Then Cecilia remembered the party after the naming ceremony. That must be it, she thought.

"Did you have anything to drink at your party, Segun?" she asked gently.

"Yes Doctor, we had to entertain our families and friends properly."

"That is not what I am asking. I am asking if you had anything to drink. Beer maybe?"

There was a pause then Segun answered, "Not

beer, Doctor, I can't afford beer."

"Then any other alcohol, Segun?" Cecilia persisted. He stood silently before her, not meeting her eyes.

"Palm wine, perhaps?"
Segun hung his head.

"Ah!" She had her answer, "Perhaps you had rather a lot on such a happy occasion?" she continued.

"I don't remember, Doctor," He sounded a little trucculent.

"I'm not accusing you Segun. But I am blaming you for not thinking about your responsibilities. However, as I have over-all responsibility for these experiments I have taken the blame." She looked sternly at Segun's relieved face. "I am sure that you know as well as I do that the Group Leader would have instantly dismissed you."

Segun prostrated in front of Cecilia, "Thank you Doctor, thank you." He rose to his feet, "I'll never let you down again, never."

Looking into his earnest eyes Cecilia knew that he meant it. "Very well Segun, I'll say no more about it. Go back to your work now."

It wasn't until Cecilia got home late that night, totally exhausted, that she allowed herself to think about herself and Ezeilo. Going to bed without any supper, for food would have choked her, she lay tossing and turning into the small hours, the events of the last two days going round and round in her baffled head. She laughed ironically to herself

216

when she thought how she had left the flat that morning determined to be cool. Well, she had met an Ezeilo far colder than she could ever be.

It was not only her professional pride that had been hurt: that he could believe that she would be so negligent, made her tender, bruised heart bleed. How could he believe that of her? Of one thing she was certain. She had been right to conclude he didn't love her. How could he have been so furiously angry with someone he loved? Her heart argued that he could, that he was the sort of man that would allow no preferential treatment, even to his wife, should she be working under him. But she daren't let one jot of hope enter her mind, or she knew she would never be able to keep up the cold facade she must do, until she left.

She couldn't help thinking how much she liked it here, both the challenge of the work and the company of her new friends. How the outlook for her future had changed since her arrival here a comparatively short time ago! She felt that she would never be so happy and carefree again.

But Cecilia's heart would not let her sleep until she had re-lived every tender moment of the night before. Remembering, she marvelled that such a rock-hard character as Ezeilo could be so unbelievably loving and gentle.

When she did fall into a troubled sleep, her pillow was dry. She had sworn never to shed another tear over Ezeilo, or any man, and she

217

intended to stick to her resolution through thick and thin.

In the ensuing week he came to her office many times, but apart from work, she would not listen to a word he had to say. There was not a chink in her steely armour and that was how she intended it to stay. Only a fool left herself open to be hurt a second time.

She showed a brave happy face to the world. She knew that the news of her broken engagement to Tim was all over the campus by now, and the last thing she wanted was for anyone to feel sorry for her. She spent a lot of her free time with Nike's children, taking them off their mother's hands as much as she could, for Nike was now having a miserable time with what she diagnosed as 'All day sickness." She was very grateful to Cecilia, while Cecilia found their childish gaiety and innocence a panacea for her unhappy heart. She would pick them up from Nike at the weekends and take them to stay with her. This way, she was not so likely to bump into Ezeilo. Although as the weeks went by, he stopped trying to break through her icy reserve and became as cold and impersonal with her as she was with him. It was relief in a way. Whatever they had between them before, it was as if it had never been. They were simply two colleagues, strangers to each other but for the job in hand. He did not refer to her resignation and neither did she, although she found it strange that Doctor Wagner had not referred to it, but then, he had been out of the country a lot.

Apart from Nike's children, Cecilia had kept away from her friends. Tête a têtes with Nike or Megan she avoided lest she should be tempted to pour out her troubles, and her pride forbade her to do that. Strangely enough it was Merribel whom she saw quite a lot of. Often when she came to visit Tim she popped up to see Cecilia and the two had become good friends. They were such opposites that Cecilia supposed that was the attraction between them. Merribel had the ability to lift her spirits with the carefree-ness of youth combined with her radiant happiness. If the other girl was aware of how desperately unhappy Cecilia was, she gave no sign, neither did she ask questions.

As for Tim, he had taken one look at her face when he first saw her after the fateful night, and knew that everything had gone terribly wrong. After a brief, "I'm so sorry,' 'he never referred to the subject again. He knew better than to do that with her in her present mood.

Nike was aware that something was terribly wrong for Cecilia. Her friend's face, always with an over-bright smile on it that never reached her eyes, was looking grey and drawn. The lovely eyes were even bigger, but dull and lifeless. If Nike had been herself she would not have let the matter rest, but would have poked and pried until she had found out the truth, in a true desire to help Cecilia. But most of her time was spent in a desperate struggle to keep her food down. Dolapo reported that Ezeilo, who harldy ever went round in the evenings now on the pretext of work, was becoming impossible.

One evening when he came back from work, Dolapo complained to Nike, "That man is working much too hard. He never leaves his room until after ten at night. Dedication is all very well, I'm all for it, but his is ridiculous. He'll have a breakdown if he isn't careful. The atmosphere in our team is terrible. Everybody is at each other's throats. I wish that man would get married, then he might give us some peace."

"Mmmm," said Nike thoughtfully, who strangely enough was not feeling sick for once." You have probably hit on the answer – for both of them. Dolapo looked puzzled, "Both of them?" he queried. His wife nodded like a wise owl. "Both of them." she answered, but was not to be drawn further.

Dropping in on Nike briefly one morning on her way back from the test fields, Cecilia accepted a cup of coffee.

"I can't thank you enough for having the children so often," Nike said as she proffered some biscuits to her friend.

"It's my pleasure, I think they are terrific kids. By the way," she continued as she refused a biscuit with a shake of her head, "what's all this about a swimming gala? I have been hearing of nothing else from Seyi and Bisi."

"You're not the only one," Nike answered with feeling, sipping her glass of water gingerly. "It's held every year and a great thing is made of it. Afterwards there is a barbecue supper for the kids. They really look forward to it. You should go, you'll enjoy it."

"Don't worry, Seyi and Bisi have said that they will only be able to stay the weekend if I can take them to the gala." Cecilia smiled at her friend.

"What cheek! I hope you put them well and truly in their places," Nike said who at the same time heaved a sigh of relief. "Seriously though, could you? I was thinking that I should have to get there somehow. Dolapo will be there, but he is helping. . ." She stopped suddenly, then went on quickly, "He always helps with the races and things, so he is too busy to keep an eye on the kids. I usually get into my swimming costume and sit there with my eyes glued to my own children. When there are as many in the water at the same time as in some of the races, anything could happen.

"Don't you worry yourself, love, I'll look after them for you. Do me good to relax by the pool." Nike looked critically at her friend, "Yes, you are rather peeky." She tried nibbling a biscuit, "I'm so hungry. It's awful, but everything I eat seems to upset me" she continued plaintively.

"You poor thing. You do have a bad time. But

surely not all the time?" Cecilia felt very sorry for her friend.

"I should say not! I wouldn't survive if it went on for nine months. No, I reckon another week or ten days should see me improving." She cheered up at the thought. "Talking of health," she continued casually, watching Cecilia through half-closed lids, "Dolapo says Ezeilo is losing weight and is like a bear with a sore head. He says that he thinks he is heading for a nervous break-down. He hasn't been round here for ages." She took another nibble, before adding, "Must be love."

For a moment Cecilia's heart lifted with hope, but it didn't last." It's true he is thinner, and more impossible than ever but the last thing that could be wrong with him is that," she said, unaware of the depth of feeling with which she uttered the words.

"You've lost weight yourself." Again Nike watched her friend closely, and seeing the bitter tightening of her lovely mouth quickly added, "but then even I have."

"I can see," Cecilia was glad to be on a safe topic once more. "You are hardly eating anything, the children tell me."

"I'm thinner at the moment, but it won't last. It will soon all be back again with a vengeance." She sounded quite cheerful at the thought.

Cecilia glanced at the watch on her slim wrist, and jumped to her feet, "Gosh! I must fly, I've got a new experiment underway that I'm watching most carefully."

"I admire your dedication to duty, I really do."

"More than I can say for some people," Cecilia replied bitterly.

"Oh dear, don't tell me that you have been catching it from Ezeilo."

"Who hasn't," Cecilia replied easily. She could not bear to tell anyone of that hateful scene over the incubator, not even Nike.

When Cecilia had left, Nike sat ruminating for a long time. She was convinced right down to the bottom of her romantic heart, that Cecilia and Ezeilo were suffering from the same ailment — unrequited love. Sadly she could not think of a thing to do about it at the moment, they were both as dangerous as prickly pears. It was impossible to get near them.

Cecilia's work kept her sane, for the whole project was really getting off the ground. With a bit of luck she would be producing millions of predators, and even see the plane in action before her six months' notice was up. At least then she would feel she had made some contribution to stave off the threatened world famine.

Despite her unhappy emotional state, the scientist in her rose to meet and conquer any snag that she hit in her part of the program. She also made frequent visits to the site of the "factory," with Butch, whose job it was to liase with the architects. Many of her ideas were incorporated in the plans. She noticed that she had won over the magnetic locks! She attended Ezeilo's weekly progress report meetings, strain though it was, and acquitted herself well. She was determined that he should not have a chance to fault her ever again. But she was not only a scientist; she was very much a flesh and blood woman, and often in the privacy of her lonely bed, she longed to be in his arms once more. If he had been able to walk in on her at these moments, her pride would have been as dust the moment he took her in his arms. But he never tried to see her off the job. Even Tim had stopped knocking on her door in the evenings as he had done the first few weeks after World Night.

She herself had become quite a hermit, excusing herself from all parties and functions. She even refused Mrs Wagner's invitations for fear that that kind lady would make her lose her iron control and she would break down in tears on her motherly breast, telling all.

So it was with surprise and pleasure that her friends greeted her when she turned up at the pool, Seyi and Bisi in tow, on the afternoon of the swimming gala.

She met Megan in the changing room. She was one of the officials, she told Cecilia, as they both slipped out of their clothes and into bikinis.

"I'm afraid I'm being lazy, I'm just looking after Nike's children for her. I've left them in the paddling pool, but I mustn't be long," Cecilia said, taking her towel out of the beach bag.

"I'm surprised Ezeilo hasn't raked you in to help." Megan picked up her towel and the two girls walked towards the showers.

"Ezeilo?" Cecilia questioned, her heart turning over, "What has he got to do with it?"

"He only organises the whole thing," Megan put her towel down and stood under the shower.

"Of course, I might have known. He's such a favourite of the children when he's in the pool. But funny that Nike never mentioned it." Cecilia too got under the shower.

"She's feeling so sick these days it probably puts everything else out of her mind," Megan replied, turning off the shower. "Almost puts you off having babies, doesn't it?"

Cecilia shook her head, "Nothing will put me off when the time comes," she said firmly but so sadly, that Megan looked at her strangely.

Cecilia did not entirely believe that Nike had been too sick to remember that Ezeilo was organising the gala. Knowing her friend, she smelt a rat. Well, it wouldn't do any good, she thought to herself determinedly, as with head held high she went out to meet whatever the afternoon had in store.

Oddly enough, she found herself thoroughly enjoying the fun and excitement of the afternoon. Ezeilo obviously intended it to be a great afternoon for the children. He worked ceaselessly, the harsh lines that were so constantly on his face these days, softened by his love of children. His body was as magnificent as ever, although a little leaner. Cecilia couldn't prevent her eyes from wandering over that never-to-be-forgotten body that had aroused feelings in her own, beyond her wildest imaginings. Once he glanced up and caught her looking at him. Their eyes met and held for an instant, an instant in which they were remembering so much. Then he looked away and it was as if the moment had never been, except that Cecilia could feel the blood rushing right up to the roots of her hair.

Finally, as the sun was getting low on the horizon, Ezeilo called through the megaphone, "Children out of the pool, please, and to the changing rooms at the double. Now parents, you must be hot and stickly, into the pool to freshen up to face the rest of the party. Those of you in swimming costumes only, of course." Amidst the laughter that greeted the latter statement, he set actions to words and putting the megaphone down, dived into the pool himself.

It was too inviting for Cecilia to resist, and so many of the parents were going into the water that she too dived in. She thought she was safe, but Ezeilo must have seen her in her turquoise and white striped bikini, for suddenly she felt a hard masculine body against her own, as a hand came round her waist to capture one firm breast. She grasped and swallowed water and came up spluttering, eyes flashing. She turned on him like a virago.

"Take your hands off me Doctor Obi. You disgust me!"

He held her for a moment before shrugging his shoulders and releasing her, "I don't know what's got into you, Lia. You have built an iron wall around yourself, and all because I was justly angry with you."

It was too much for Cecilia, "Justly angry? Do you really think that I was capable of carelessness like that?" her eyes flashed. "You'll never ..." she stopped suddenly, her face becoming dull and expressionless, "There's no point in carrying on this conversation," she said wearily, in a cold voice. "We have nothing to say to each other." She turned her back on him and climbed out of the pool, wishing that she could just go home and forget about the barbecue.

Luckily, it turned out that she could, for Dolapo said he was free to look after Ṣeyi and Bisi now. Both of whom had had a lovely time. Seyi had won his heat in the relay, and Bisi had won her 'once across the width of the bath' race.

Cecilia found it hard to sleep that night: the touch of Ezeilo's body had set her aflame and she realised that she was just as hopelessly in love with him as ever.

The firm resolution that she had made so bravely, and the pent up longing to lie once again in his arms that she had kept, surpressed, crumbled in the face of her deep unhappiness, with memories of the touch of his strong body which had weakned her resolve. She wished with all her tender heart that she had never gone to the gala. Tears streamed unheeded down her lovely sad face, as she tried to go to sleep.

Chapter Ten

The following Monday evening, Cecilia was climbing the stairs to her apartment when Tim's door opened, and he took her arm saying, "You're to come in and have supper with me Cecilia — please."

She made to protest but Tim said firmly, "I won't take no for an answer. You look all in, and I have cooked a delicious curry, though I do say it myself." There was certainly a lovely aroma floating out of the kitchen, and she gave in. It would be nice to have a quiet dinner with Tim.

"Thank you, I'd like that. I'm far too tired to begin to cook anything for myself tonight anyway." Tim looked at her disapprovingly. "Don't think I hadn't noticed." He sat her down in a chair overlooking the lake and went to fetch her a drink.

"Where's Merribel tonight?" Cecilia asked Tim, for she was usually there in the evening.

"Her parents wanted her to help entertain some guests of theirs." Tim handed her a cool drink. "It's vodka and tonic. I know you drink them occasionally and you look as if a drink would do you good. "

"Oh dear! Do I really look that bad?"

Tim put his own drink on the occasional table between them and looked kindly at her ravaged face. "Let's say that I have seen you look a lot better."

She gave him a tremulous smile, tears glistening in her eyes, "Does it show so much?" she asked. Tim smiled gently in return, "Maybe only to me who knows you so well," he said rising to his feet. "Hang on a minute, I have forgotten to stir the rice, back in a jiffy."

Cecilia sat back, letting the calmness of the moonlight on the lake soothe her ragged nerves. "I'm glad you are so happy, Tim" she said brightly on his return.

"Thanks to you. You were always braver and stronger than I. I think that is one of the things that was wrong between us. Merribel is such a helpless little creature that she makes me feel ten feet tall."

"Am I a very arrogant woman, then?" Cecilia asked, a touch of sadness in her face.

Tim shook his head, "You were never arrogant. You just have more brains and more character than most, and it shows. You should be proud of it." Tim finished his drink and stood up to get another. "For instance," he continued. "I'm going to have another drink , although I know I shouldn't. You wouldn't do that."

"But I have, Tim, I have, and something much worse than having a drink when I shouldn't have," she cried, and suddenly she was pouring out the whole story to the one person she knew would never sit in judgement. It was a tremendous relief to share the almost unbearable burden of unhappiness she had born alone for so long. There was silence in the room when Cecilia finally finished her tale of woe. Looking across at Tim's sad expression, she whispered, "I'm sorry Tim if it has hurt you.

Your idol has feet of clay, you see," she ended miserably. Tim took her hands in his, saying "I wouldn't be human if I were not just a little piqued that Ezeilo comes along and can sweep you off your feet into his bed in a matter of a few short weeks, while I could never get you there." He gave her a little grin.

"But you always played fair. He used every means at his disposal and was totally ruthless," she replied hotly.

"Maybe I would have got farther with you if I had had a bit more of Ezeilo's ruthlessness and drive." He looked seriously at Cecilia, as he stroked her hand." I'm deadly serious, love. You need a strong over bearing man like Ezeilo because you are such a strong character yourself."

"Oh, Tim!" she couldn't help smiling, "now you are talking like a real chauvinist."

231

"I'm all for women's lib in the office or anywhere that men and women are employed together. You know that. But when it comes down to the Adam and Eve bit, I firmly believe that every woman likes her man to be the boss." He looked sheepishly down at his hands. "And with Merribel I am definitely that."

Lucky Tim, and clever Merribel, Cecilia thought, for she knew that Merribel was by no means as helpless as she let Tim think. "I wish I were more like Merribel. Maybe then Ezeilo would love me," she sighed.

Tim looked at her curiously, "What makes you so sure that he doesn't. He has all the signs of a man crossed in love, to me."

"Because he's after one thing, and one thing only, where women are concerned — no involvement. Doesn't his behaviour with me prove that what I am saying is true?" Cecilia said flatly.

Tim shook his head. "Not necessarily. You are as cold as an iceberg when he is anywhere near. My bet is that you have frozen him off, after that unfortunate episode of the incubator."

"How could he believe that of me?" Cecilia asked Tim the question that had tortured her over the last few weeks.

"You know what a complex man he is, and how dedicated to his work. Put yourself in his place for a moment. Rightly or wrongly, he has a firm belief that women with emotional entanglements are

232

unreliable. Not only did he think you were engaged to me but on top of that he himself was pressurising you to break with me. Isn't that compounding the very thing that he is so sure will make you unreliable?" He looked at her earnestly, "I'm no psychiatrist, but thinking as he does, he is conditioned to believe the worst about you, and on top of that he feels guilty, as he had been one of the contributing factors. Am I making sense?" Cecilia nodded, intent on his words. "And," continued Tim, "it is more than possible, being the dedicated man that he is, that he was more furious with himself than you. Another cause of his unreasona-bleness." Tim rose to his feet, with a smile, "Can you make head or tail of that? I fear I must go and dish up the curry before it is over-cooked. And anyway, I am sure he wouldn't have felt so guilty about it all, if he hadn't been in love you." With that he left her to her own devices and disappeared into the kitchen.

Cecilia had never thought of it from that angle before. She had been too involved with her own emotions and too hurt by Ezeilo's actions to be able to see clearly. She felt a thin thread of hope filtering through her veins, as her reason told her that there was a possibility it could be as her heart wished it to be.

She had always known that Ezeilo was a difficult and complex man. Hadn't that been part of his attraction, as much as his devasting looks and physique? A little fire deep inside her being, started to melt the icy barrier round her heart. She was frightened to hope — hardly dare to — but as Tim put it to her later over the curry, what had she to lose? Only her unhappiness.

She ate the heartiest meal that she had eaten for weeks, and Tim was pleased to see a little life back in her face again.

"I wouldn't have left you alone with him that night, if I hadn't thought that you both cared for each other. I thought you just needed a little push in the right direction." He gave her another helping of fruit salad. "But I must confess when I saw your face the next evening, I feared I had made a terrible mistake. But you were as tight as a drum. I hardly dared say that I was sorry."

"Oh dear! Am I so frightening?"

Tim shook his head reassuringly, "You're not a bit frightening, but you feel very passionately about things. The trouble is you hide it, control yourself with a rod of iron." He took her face gently in his hands. "Whatever comes of it all, you will always owe Ezeilo a debt of gratitude."

"Gratitude?"

Tim nodded, "For making you face up to the fact that you are a very passionate and emotional lady. Something that I would never have guessed in a thousand years — and I thought I knew you," he added ruefully.

"I'm sorry Tim, truly sorry." Cecilia's eyes gazed

earnestly into his.

"I'm not, and you mustn't be either. You and I were not right for each other, but I think that you and he are. "He placed a chaste kiss on her forhead," I want you to be as happy as Merribel and I are, you and Ezeilo."

"Dear Tim," Cecilia said, affectionately. "You'll never know what you've done for me tonight. I wish I had confided in you earlier."

"You mightn't have listened to me then. You seem to have let your defences down tonight. You aren't so impregnable as you were."

Cecilia nodded, "You're quite right. I never realised how observant you are." There was a real warmth between them. Tim hesitated for a moment and then said haltingly, "I meant everything I said to you about being ambitious, and believing in making the right kind of friends in high places. I'll still do it, and Merribel will help me, but I would want Merribel for my wife whoever her parents were. You do believe that, don't you?"

Cecilia squeezed his arm. "Of course I do. It stands out a mile that you are besotted with her." She rose to her feet. "And now I must go to bed if I am to be up before the lizards." She put her arms round his neck. "Good night, dear Tim, and thank you for everything." She kissed him gently on the mouth before walking to the door to mount the stairs to her own place, a considerably more cheerful person than a couple of hours.

Nevertheless in the ensuing weeks, nothing seemed changed between herself and Ezeilo. Try as she might she could not bring herself to walk into his office, and just out of the blue, say she loved him. She wasn't even positive that Tim's conjectures were accurate. And what if he really didn't love her and still only wanted her body? It wasn't easy to wipe away all the fears and doubts of weeks, just because Tim had given her some reason to hope. She decided that she would look for a crack in Ezeilo's armour and when and if she found it, then, only then, given the faintest glimmer of hope, she would fling her arms round his neck and brazenly admit her love for him. No foolish pride would stop her then. But she decided that she must have that one glimmer. So she steeled herself to wait patiently for the slightest sign that he cared about her.

Gradually the hope in her heart withered and died, as Ezeilo was as impersonal as ever. He too had erected a barrier and she could not scale its heights. Her spirits sank to their lowest ebb, until she longed for her six months to come to an end so that she could get away from his physical presence and try to forget him.

She realised over the weeks, that important as her work was to her, his love was far more important. Without him, she was nothing. She began to do her work automatically, her pride keeping her up to scratch, but there was no more joy in it for her.

The time came for her to release some parasitoids on the cassava in the experimental fields on the periphery of the campus. This would be the final experiment before the arrival of the plane that was going to do the real job. It had been decided at the last weekly meeting, that she should do it that week. She collected the parasitoids from the control greenhouse, her gum boots and straw hat from her office and strode down to her car. She should just have time before the twelve o'clock siren went.

It was a hot day, with very little wind and the sun was beating down brightly as Cecilia set about her work. The fields were deserted except for herself. She released a few thousand parasitoids at various strategic places, going deeper into the field as she did so. Concentrating on the job in hand she had just released yet another few thousand parasitoids when a slight noise made her look down. She froze to the spot, as a sinister spitting cobra raised it's flat head, it's cold eyes upon Cecilia. She didn't know what to do. Her gum boots she knew would not protect her. Not from a spitting cobra. Sweat poured down her face and her whole body started to shake as she and the snake stood there looking at each other. Suddenly, like a miracle, she heard Ezeilo's voice calling her name. But try as she might she could not answer nor take her eyes off the snake.

There was a sudden silence as Ezeilo's voice stopped calling. Please let him not go away. Please!' She sent a fervent prayer up to her Maker. As if in answer to her prayer, a shot shattered the silence in the field, and her unbelieving eyes saw the snake sink to the ground, where it writhed horribly for a few moments before it was still. The world began to spin round and as Cecilia began to fall to the ground in a dead faint, strong arms caught her and held her close.

She came round to find herself in Ezeilo's arms, his kisses on her throat. He held her as if he would never let her go. "Oh my love, my poor little love. What if I had lost you! I cannot endure our separation a moment longer. I will make you love me, as I love you. Not with brute force. I will not thrust my selfish desire on you my darling. I have made many mistakes in the past, but forgive me, my love, and I will woo you with a love as ardent and passionate as you desire, no less, no more." Looking deeply into his eyes, so near her own, Cecilia saw his words of love mirrored in their vibrant gaze. She gave a little sigh of pure happiness, then, eyes shimmering with un-shed tears of joy, she put an arm round his neck pulling his head down to hers. Their kiss was long and profound, he holding back his passion, until the passion of her lips told him all he needed to know. There was no need for wooing – she loved him as much as he loved her.

Much later, when they were seated close together on his sofa, Cecilia asked a question that had been puzzling her. "How, my darling, did you know that I was out in the fields, and how did you happen to have a gun on you?" she said gaving a little shudder as she thought of what could have happened had he not come to her rescue.

Feeling her shiver, Ezeilo pulled her close. "One of the field hands came and reported that he had disturbed a family of cobras in the cassava field. I went to your office to warn you, only to find that you were not there.

It was Segun who said that you had already gone. Segun, for whom you took the blame! How I have wronged you, and all the time I loved you so."

"It doesn't matter, darling, not any more." He kissed her passionately, then continued, "You'll never know the agony I went through, thinking that I might have sent you to your death. Or at least blinded. I picked up the revolver I keep for emergencies and followed you just as fast as I could. Thank God I was in time. When you just stood there like a frozen statue, not answering my call, I knew what was the matter. You had told me you were petrified of snakes, remember, on that fateful day in Abeokuta."

Cecilia nodded, "Was it there that you fell in love with me?" she asked, shyly.

Ezeilo shook his head, "I fell in love with you when you were so annoyed with me on the plane, my little spitfire." He stopped her reply with a kiss. It was sometime before they spoke again and they

239

were both breathless.

"It was so difficult for me, being engaged . . . . ."
Cecilia began.

"A fact which you kept impressing on me, my
sweet, with infuriating regularity."

"I felt so guilty you see and . . ."
Once more he stopped her mouth with kisses, "I
was a brute to you, my darling, I shall never forgive
myself," he said penitently a few minutes later,
"and I committed the terrible sin of taking your
virginity so cruelly. Can you ever forgive me, my
little intellectual?"

Her nickname was now a term of endearment to
Cecilia, no longer a source of irritation. "I can
forgive you that, but why, oh why did you never
say you loved me?" Cecilia asked softly.

He held her away from him a minute, "But I told
you with my body. Surely you felt the same uplifting
of your spirit and I did, when we consumated our
love?" Cecilia smiled, a woman's smile, as she
answered, "We females are a nuisance, I know, but
we must hear the words before we can really believe
that we are truly loved." She ran her fingers down
his cheek as she spoke.

"Then I shall make up for it, my little doubting
Thomasina, by saying over and over again in your
little shell-like ear, I love you. I love you. I love
you. Will that do?" Ezeilo asked as he kissed each
eye-lid tenderly.

Cecilia shook her head as she looked at him, all

the love in her heart shining out of her eyes. There was a pause, and then, a tender smile playing about his lips Ezeilo said softly, "Will you please marry me?"

Cecilia gave a sigh of utter contentment, and with her whole countenance illuminated with joy, she said, "Oh, yes! My beloved chauvinist"

With a sardonic lift of one eyebrow, he pulled her closer to his chest in a very masterly fashion.

SPECTRUM PAPERBACKS